Girl at Dunkirk

By David Spiller

Copyright © 2017 by David Spiller

Also by David Spiller:

Pilot Error

Out of Burma

Very short stories

Bridger's Diary – a Mozart fantasy

(Available on Amazon)

Girl at Dunkirk

~ One ~

Chrissie walked quickly home from work. She was late and her mother would be fretting about dinner, and it couldn't be helped. A girl who'd left school at 15 with no qualifications had to grab the chances that came her way. She was grateful for her job at Arter & Co, the Morris service department, and if they asked her to handle a late rush job that's what she did. They'd taken her on for a pittance at 18 because she'd gone round there twice a week pestering the manager for work. Three years later he was glad to have her and she got paid properly; and her sex was no longer an issue because he knew and she knew she was the best of the three young mechanics at the garage.

There was no distance to speak of between her home and Arter's place, but in any case Chrissie always went on foot when out and about in Ramsgate. She'd not ridden on one of the new motor buses – or on the old tram system – since she was thirteen. For that matter she'd not used the lift that took people from the sandy beach up to the cliff top.

The pavements were crammed with May holiday-makers, despite the gloomy speculation that had oppressed the country since Britain's declaration of war the previous September. Was real war on the way, or not? No-one seemed to know. Many thought it would all be over before Christmas. Even so Ramsgate had changed in the preceding six months: rationing, khaki in the streets, the unnatural dearth of children following evacuation, the rule about taking your gas mask into picture houses (which had discouraged her from seeing *The road to Singapore* the previous week). She'd noticed other things too. There were sandbags in the streets but no bombs (though a German plane had recently crashed upon Clacton and destroyed 50 houses). And their Italian greengrocer, Gallo's, had a card in the shop window – 'We are British citizens, please buy from us'.

Walking in Ramsgate, Chrissie felt both affection and irritation for the town where she'd grown up. She loved the sound and sight of the sea and the pervasive salt aroma. She quite liked the gulls, though a lot of people didn't. She flinched from the celebrated sandy beaches when they were clogged with trippers, but revelled in the Marina Bathing Pool, which was open to the elements with vistas of cliffs above and the sea beyond. She recoiled utterly from the three miles of 'Ramsgate Tunnels', recently excavated from the cliffs to shelter inhabitants during the air raids that hadn't happened. An entrance to this network lay close to her home, but nothing would have persuaded Chrissie into the tunnel system's musty confines; she'd rather be blown to pieces in the open air.

She arrived at her home now, number 150 High Street, a small, 3-up 3-down house in a scruffy brick terrace. She walked through to the cramped living room.

'You've got oil on your face,' said her mother, whose opening remark was invariably some form of complaint.

'It's the work, mother. I've been attending to a sump.'

Mrs Sellick sniffed. 'I don't doubt it.'

Chrissie shot a look at her father, who was reading *The News Chronicle* in an armchair. 'At least it's easier to clean up now,' she said. Removing grease had been a problem for both Chrissie and her father – a machine tool engineer – when the house only had cold water. Now they had an Ascot and *hot* water. Her mother would have preferred one of the new washing machines on the never-never, but they couldn't afford both.

'Then go and clean up, girl,' Mrs Sellick said. 'The meal's spoiling.'

Chrissie went into the scullery and removed her blouse, belatedly remembering to draw the curtain that shielded her half-naked body from view. She could hear sounds of the dinner being removed from the oven. Splashing about in the sink, chastising her skin with a scrubbing brush, she reflected for the umpteenth time on the lack of patience in her own character. She'd had no previous experience of sickness and was proving, in that respect at least, to be a slow learner. The merest glance at her mother reinforced the need for forbearance. Mrs Sellick's features were customarily shadowed with discontent but there was a new element now, a compression of lips betraying pain brought by the cancer.

' I'm sorry, mum,' Chrissie muttered under her breath, 'I'm so sorry.'

Back in the dining room, food was on the table. Chrissie took her seat, still fastening the blouse.

'That's a bit better,' said her mother.

'I'm as fresh as a daisy now,' Chrissie responded.

Her father had chosen this moment to divest himself of one pullover and wriggle into another.

'Wally, do you have to?' said his wife.

'I've got to be just right, Molly – you know that.'

It was true; Mr Sellick had a lifelong habit of adjusting his dress to suit minor changes of temperature, to his wife's abiding irritation. Trying – for once – to side with her mother, Chrissie observed 'If you were in khaki, dad, you'd have to put up with what the Army gave you,' and immediately regretted the remark. Her father's call-up rejection on health grounds had been a bitter blow to him. She made as if to touch his arm, without actually doing so. 'Sorry, dad. Actually I'm really glad you're *not* in uniform. It means no-one can shoot at you.'

Her father grunted and they ate in silence for a while, a familiar scene. Trying to change the subject, Chrissie said 'There's no news, I suppose?'

Her mother glared. 'Of course there isn't.'

The enquiry could only have referred to one thing. Chrissie's older brother Tom was a naval rating. He'd been out of touch for the past two months and conversation in the house often dwelt on his whereabouts. The big fear was that he'd been posted to Norway. Not that they had any firm information, but rumour suggested the Norway operation hadn't gone well. They dreaded the thought of a telegram being delivered to their front door.

'I don't want news, thank you,' Mr Sellick said. 'You know what they say about "no news".'

'There's no point to news in wartime,' said his wife. 'It's all lies. You have to find out from someone who knows someone.'

'Which is where your ludicrous brother comes in,' said Mr Sellick. 'Or could do if he wanted to.'

'Stephen can't talk about his work,' replied Mrs Sellick. 'You know that. A word in the wrong place would get him into trouble.'

'There are ways of handling that sort of thing.'

'He can't talk and that's that.'

It was one of many subjects best avoided at 150 High Street. 'Uncle Stephen' had an important job – or so he told them – at the naval base in Dover. He'd have known a good deal about current events but would never let on, beyond dropping tantalising hints ('You don't know the half of it, Wally'). But the reason for discord between the two men lay deeper. Chrissie's mother and Uncle Stephen had enjoyed a middle class upbringing, whereas her father had (as he liked to insist) 'an impeccable working class background'. Mrs Sellick's 'hoity toity aspirations' (Mr Sellick's phrase again), encouraged by brother Stephen, didn't fit with a rented terraced house in Ramsgate.

That wasn't all. Regarding her parents now across the dinner table, Chrissie couldn't imagine how they'd ever come together; ever climbed into the sack for long enough to generate herself and Tom. In most important respects they were chalk and cheese: her mother a confirmed Conservative voter, her father an outspoken, troublesome socialist whose hero was J B Priestley; her mother a regular church-goer, her father a confirmed atheist. Whenever the pair tried to communicate, their beliefs and prejudices got in the way. It was worse without Tom in the house, because he'd had the knack of molllifying both parents.

Chrissie on the other hand was – all too clearly – her father's child, with the same unholy beliefs. So why wasn't he more demonstrative with her, she eternally wondered; why not confide in her, recognise the bond that – he surely realised – could have flourished. In her view she got the worst of both worlds.

'I suppose Tom *could* be in France,' said Chrissie. 'In a ship lying off the coast.'

'Don't talk daft, girl,' said her mother.

'What do you think, dad?'

Mr Sellick shook his head. 'I can't see a role for the navy over there. Not now the troops are already in France.' He scoffed. '*British Expeditionary Force*, my foot. Damn ridiculous sending hundreds of thousands of our men to the continent.'

'Why do you say that?' his daughter asked.

'They're not doing anything, are they, as far as we know? Besides, we're an island. That's our strength. We want our men here. Whereas in France...' He leaned both elbows on the table, which never failed to annoy his wife. 'Would you want your safety to depend upon the Froggies?'

'Don't know, dad – I've only met them here in Ramsgate. They've got that line thing, haven't they? All those pill boxes along their border.'

'The Maginot Line. And tell me, my sweet, why do they have that there?'

'Don't know, dad.'

'Because they don't fancy doing their fighting on French territory, that's why.'

'Oh!'

'Yes "oh!" - you think about that, girl.'

'Don't worry,' Mrs Sellick told her. 'Churchill will sort things out.' Winston Churchill had become Prime Minister ten days earlier – 11th May, 1940. 'He knows what he's doing.'

Mr Sellick snorted. 'Chamberlain, Churchill...one useless Tory bugger after another.'

'Please don't swear, Wally.'

'Churchill might be a dab hand with a cigar or a whisky and soda. A war, on the other hand...'

It was familiar territory, but Chrissie still asked. 'What don't you like about him, dad?'

'I'll tell you what. He's crossed the floor of the house twice, Chrissie. Not once, twice. Tory to Liberal, then back to Tory again. What does that suggest? They wouldn't have him in the Labour party, I tell you that.'

'Don't be absurd Wally,' said Mrs Sellick. 'Churchill's from the aristocracy.'

Chrissie slipped away from the table. 'Thanks for the dinner, mum. Sorry I have to run. Got to smarten myself up.'

Three evenings a week she worked behind the bar at the Tavern in Vale Road. The landlord liked to have young women on duty, and considering she came home covered in grease, Chrissie could scrub up quite well when she wanted to. She had good breasts and dressed to put them discreetly on show, because it brought in the customers. She knew how to flirt with the men but not so they could take liberties, all of which the landlord also liked. In fact she had gone out with a man she first met in the Tavern – he'd taken her greyhound racing at Dumpton Park – but though she liked going out, she didn't really care for him. She'd let him kiss her a couple of times.

When she ended her shift at the Vale Tavern that evening she took a detour to walk back by the harbour road. It felt good to clear her head, to expel the punters' cigarette smoke from her lungs. A breeze had blown up and the sea displayed crazy reflections of the moon. Few people were about after eleven and she strode along the front wishing she could follow her favourite route. Since the declaration of war the Admiralty had taken over the harbour, which put the Sailors' Church out of bounds. Normally Chrissie wasn't one for churches; she wouldn't be seen dead in her mother's place of worship, the claustrophobic St George's, hemmed in by mouldering grave stones. But the Sailors' Church – a simple, rectangular building next to vertiginous diagonal steps up the cliff – was her favourite place in Ramsgate. She happened to have been down there a month earlier. The church had a tradition of looking after sailors in trouble, and survivors were taken there when the S S Lulworth was mined off Ramsgate. Chrissie had been summoned to help because she'd done the Red Cross course in first aid.

She stopped and leaned against the harbour wall, staring wistfully across the water. What she especially resented about the war was losing the most treasured thing in her world. On many weekends she and her father had been along the coast in their motor yacht, *Blithe Spirit*, the bane of her mother's life, the cause (Mrs Sellick insisted) of further self-sacrifice, notwithstanding that it was owned jointly with one of her father's workmates. Of course since the declaration of war, using personal pleasure craft was out of the question, and Chrissie's pride and joy had been locked away in a ramshackle boat-house (a further expense for her mother to rail at).

She stared into the darkness, out past the harbour wall to the sea beyond. In daylight, when the weather was clear, you could sometimes see across the channel to France. Somewhere beyond that surprisingly narrow stretch of water were the British troops; not Tom, it seemed, but a multitude of men who her father thought should never have gone out there at all – men who were supposed to be fighting, but were apparently loafing about in the so-called 'phony war'. It struck her that within a few hours she and her father *could* – though they'd never done it – take *Blithe Spirit* across the Channel to the French coast and see what was going on. At that moment the place seemed intimately close. The thought gave her a very strange sensation.

~ Two ~

In the week that followed Chrissie's late evening fantasy about taking the boat across to France, she learnt nothing concerning the activities of the British Expeditionary Force. In that, she was no different from the rest of the British population. There were occasional news items suggesting all was not well, like the *Daily Mail's* report that the forces in France were 'hemmed in'. But then on 26th May the Ministry of Information (often referred to by the public as 'The Ministry of Misinformation') said straight out that they could give no details about the BEF operation and Harold Nicolson, from the same source, warned against 'careless chatter'. The only regular 'news' came via the dubious broadcasts from Germany of Lord Haw Haw, which most people listened to though they pretended not to. In such circumstances rumours abounded. The most persistent one described Hitler's plans for an invasion of Britain, and it was reinforced when Anthony Eden called for the creation of a volunteer defence corps in Britain's towns. By the third week of May most Brits accepted that invasion was imminent. This rumour carried a particular force for the populations of coastal towns like Ramsgate.

During the waiting period Chrissie felt unusually on edge. Her character was built for positive action, and without information she had to sit back and wait. She considered joining the ATS, but reconsidered when someone said ATS girls were renowned for throwing themselves at men.

Then on 27th May they had an evening visit from her mother's brother, Uncle Stephen. Though he also lived in Ramsgate, this was unusual. Work in the Dover naval base took much of his time, to the extent that he often spent the night there. And the uneasy relationship with Chrissie's father discouraged 'Uncle Stephen' from social visits to 150 High Street.

This time Mrs Sellick insisted he stay for dinner, and an extra chair was placed at the dining table.

Mr Sellick opened hostilities immediately. 'So, Stephen, what's kicking off in your big-shot job – not that you're going to tell us?'

'Don't start, Wally,' said Mrs Sellick.

'We're pretty busy in Dover,' Uncle Stephen responded, 'As you can perhaps imagine'.

'What about the famous Expeditionary Force?' Mr Sellick went on. 'We never hear a dicky bird.'

Uncle Stephen had already assumed his uncooperative expression. 'Oh that's military stuff, Wally. We don't get to know the details. We're the Navy.'

'Of course you are. What about your boss – what's he like? Ramsay, isn't it?'

'Vice-Admiral Ramsay, yes. Experienced man. He's OK.'

'Only OK?'

'He retired once. Came back again two years ago. Bit of a disciplinarian. The men seem to like him.'

'You're not so sure?' Mr Sellick urged.

'I didn't say that. He tends to cut back a bit on procedure.'

'No red tape, you mean. I don't suppose you like that?'

'Everything must have its place.'

The needling followed a familiar course, but Chrissie could see where her father was coming from. Uncle Stephen was known for falling out with people. Deeply religious, he was the organist at his local church, but had already quarrelled with the vicar about the order of service. His long face, dogmatically set, was a warning that he could be difficult.

'How many of you work in the Dover office?' Mr Sellick asked.

'It's a decent-sized operation. Plenty of Wrens about, of course. Just twelve of us fellows in the senior team. Twelve plus Ramsay.'

'Oh! Like Jesus Christ and the disciples.'

'I really don't appreciate remarks of that kind.'

'Leave it out Wally,' said Mrs Sellick.

'And *where* do you work?' Mr Sellick pressed on. 'Someone told me you were actually inside the cliffs.'

'That's correct. The offices have been cut into the chalk.'

'A bit claustrophobic maybe?'

Uncle Stephen shrugged. 'Ramsay's got a window that looks out over the English Channel. The rest of us, no. I'm quite happy there. The ops room is like a white cave. There's a circular table with a big map on it.'

'That's very interesting, Stephen,' Mr Sellick said.

Uncle Stephen looked up sharply, suspecting sarcasm was behind the rare compliment.

'No really,' Mr Sellick continued. 'You've never told us so much before.'

'Actually...' The man seemed to wrestle with his conscience before taking the plunge. 'I came round to tell you something else.'

'Blimey, a field day. Well go on then. You can talk freely before all of us.'

'Um...have you ever heard the expression "Operation Dynamo",' Uncle Stephen said eventually.

'No.'

'Hm. Well never mind that. The point is, not long ago the Admiralty started collecting particulars of small boats, especially those on the Thames estuary and the Kent coast – self propelled craft from 30 to 100 feet.'

'I saw something in the papers,' said Mr Sellick. 'For mine-sweeping work, if I remember right.'

'It was at the time. The situation's changed somewhat.'

'What do you mean?'

'I can't tell you.'

Even Mrs Sellick was becoming irritated by her brother's mask of secrecy. 'Come on Stephen,' she urged. 'What *can* you tell us?'

'Look...the need for boats is becoming urgent. That's why I'm here. I'm seeing several Ramsgate people this evening. The thing is, Wally...you have a boat.'

'Well yes. I share one with a colleague. When's it likely to be needed?'

'Very soon.'

'But you know what it's like, Stephen – *you* of all people. It's been laid up in a grotty boat-house all winter. An old boat like ours, you can't just take it out and use it, hey presto. It needs care and attention. A spring overhaul for the motor, rusty parts replaced, so on and so forth. Two or three weeks work at least. You *know* that.'

Chrissie shifted in her seat. 'Um, dad...'

'Not now, Chrissie love.'

'No dad, I mean...actually I've *been* looking after her. I've *been* giving her attention.'

Father gave daughter a look, a mixture of irritation and pride.

'I know you're not supposed to but I see it as back-up for my job. I *like* messing about with mechanical stuff. I've been going round there, fine-tuning the engine. It's all OK. Don't worry, no-one knows.'

There was a silence while the others absorbed this. 'There you are then, Stephen,' said Mr Sellick eventually. 'It seems we have a boat which *is* in running order. So what might you want to do with it?'

'It's the Admiralty that wants it.'

'But what for, man?'

'I'm sorry, I still can't say.'

Mr Sellick was getting hot under the collar. Chrissie knew the signs – the way he'd started rubbing his forehead with the back of a hand. He raised his voice now. 'What a peculiar organisation you run, Stephen. You want something, but you won't say what or why. I'm surprised anything gets done in Dover at all. Well I'll tell you something. If you have my boat you get me along with it. Otherwise there's no deal.'

'That may actually be possible.' Uncle Stephen looked awkward, as well he might. 'The Admiralty wants good local men from Ramsgate. People who know the tides and the currents. Who know the Goodwins, for heaven's sake.'

'Oh we know them,' Mr Sellick agreed, about the notorious sandbanks that had confounded British shipping throughout history.

'The Admiralty could arrange a naval rating to help you,' Uncle Stephen added.

'I don't need that. I've got Jim, my co-owner. He'd be up for it, whatever "it" is.'

Stephen shook his head. 'No, you'd need three people. That'll be the minimum permitted.'

'Don't talk soft, man. Me and Chrissie have taken her up and down this coastline any number of times. It's a doddle.'

'No, Wally. Three men.'

Mrs Sellick cut short the argument by rising to collect the dinner things, ignoring Chrissie's 'Let me do that, mum'. She glared at her brother in a way that was unusual, since the pair of them normally presented a united front. Her strangled comment wafted across the table. 'I don't know how you can do this to me Stephen, on top of everything else.'

He half-rose. 'Don't be upset, Molly. It's a precautionary measure.'

She turned towards him with a bitter face. 'Don't patronise me. I know exactly what it is.'

Mr Sellick's expression as his wife swept from the room was a picture. He was often heard to remark 'Of course, my wife's more intelligent than me,' with pride rather than any other emotion, but at moments like this – when she understood something that he didn't – his feelings were mixed.

As Chrissie reached the kitchen with the rest of the dinner things she was greeted by the sound of smashing crockery. She found Mrs Sellick leaning with both arms on the sink, breathing heavily. Pieces of broken china littered the floor. Chrissie put an arm round her mother's shoulders, meeting the usual resistance.

'It's all right, mum. I'll clear up in here. You know, you really have to start taking things more easily.'

Mrs Sellick shook her head, muttering almost inaudibly, 'How could he, how could he?'

***   ***   ***

Over the next few days the scales fell from Mr Sellick's eyes and he understood what his wife had known instinctively. The media shut-down continued but the citizens of Ramsgate and other east-coast ports saw for themselves what Londoners couldn't. The evidence could hardly be misunderstood. One by one, vessels that were the worse for wear crawled into Ramsgate harbour: motor-boats, lifeboats, fishing craft, cutters. Men swarmed off their decks and out of the holds, so that it seemed hardly possible for small boats to carry so many. And what men!: dirty, bearded, grim-faced, barely able to stand, sustaining each other as they stumbled along the quay. Some went barefoot. Others had bandages stained dark with blood. The more seriously wounded got hurried away by stretcher-bearers. The Salvation Army were on hand and nurses tried to put a cheerful face on things. The most disturbing aspect was the mood that had enveloped the returnees: the sombre, lifeless humour of defeat.

Chrissie saw the scenes herself after a workmate reported what was going on. She nipped out during her lunch hour and joined people who'd massed to rubberneck on calamity. Barriers had been set up in the street to hold them back. What struck her was the stillness of the onlookers; their sullen disbelief at the portents of defeat, the end of their hopes for a short war and their fears of a grim future. The mute ranks stood three deep and she strained to see over their heads as troops were shepherded onto buses, taken along the front for refreshment in cafés. In rare moments when someone from the crowd called out, the figures in khaki made no response. Everything was silence.

This needs to change, Chrissie thought, with sudden discernment; we have to find some way of lifting people's spirits – troops and civilians alike – for all our sakes.

The returnees were only half the picture. The denizens of a harbour town are accustomed to monitoring movements by water, and Chrissie saw the first significant signs as she walked home from work on May 29th. A motor boat called *Bonny Heather* was leaving the harbour, apparently leading a convoy of small craft, each towing a ship's lifeboat. To her knowledge it was the first convoy to go from Ramsgate and it could only have been making for the French coast. She later heard that one of the boats had returned to base with engine trouble, while another broke down and made fast for the night to a Goodwin lightship.

One boat in the convoy belonged to someone she knew, and her stomach lurched uneasily at the implications of this. Even so she'd never have given credence to the events that were about to envelop her and her family. This wasn't surprising for they had no parallel in recent history.

*** *** ***

Soon after she reached home that day they had a second visitation from Uncle Stephen. They had no phone, so he had to call in when he wanted to contact them quickly. His grim expression was a harbinger of bad news. Chrissie's mother barely extended a greeting; she went straight upstairs and didn't come down till he'd left. So it was Mr Sellick who received his brother-in-law in the dining room, and Chrissie was allowed to sit in and listen.

'You may have guessed why I'm here,' the visitor began.

Mr Sellick nodded. 'There've been reports in the press today – at long last. But we hardly needed them in Ramsgate. We've seen what's happening with our own eyes. It's the Expeditionary Force, isn't it?'

Uncle Stephen pursed his lips, barely able to speak.

'They've been beaten then?' Mr Sellick insisted.

'That's about the size of it – as far as we can tell.'

'Don't you know?'

Uncle Stephen had been cautious for so long, keeping thoughts to himself, that he found it hard to confirm what was already obvious. 'It's chaos over there,' he admitted at length. 'Not that we really know. Communications on the ground are hopeless. But yes...they've lost, and now all those men – three hundred thousand plus – are blockaded on the French coast by the Germans.'

Mr Sellick banged the dining room table with his fist. 'Damn it, I knew it. *I knew it*. Crazy, crazy thing to do, sending all those troops on a wild goose chase.'

'All right, Wally, but it's no use...'

'*Please* don't talk to me about spilt milk. This was rank, bleeding stupidity.'

'Well...'

'So what now? Is that it? Have we lost the war already?'

'It's a desperate moment all right,' Uncle Stephen conceded, 'But we believe – and this goes right up to the top – that we can get some of the troops back here in the next two or three days. Fifty thousand, maybe, who knows. Better than nothing. The operation's already started.'

Mr Sellick stared at him. 'Fifty thousand! Evacuation then! You're talking evacuation?'

'Yes, that's it.'

'Just a minute. You used the words "Operation Dynamo" the other day. Is that what you were on about? Is this Dynamo we're witnessing?'

'That's right, Operation Dynamo. You mustn't repeat a word of this, Wally. Or you, Chrissie.'

'No, Uncle Stephen.'

After a moment Mr Sellick said 'Chrissie, get me your old school atlas, will you.' When she'd fetched it her father scrabbled in the pages to find the map of France. 'Right then, so whereabouts are these British troops?' he asked his brother-in-law.

'Come on, Wally, give me an easier one,' said Uncle Stephen. 'They *were* in Belgium. That much we know. They seem to be falling back to the coast in a confused rab...' He reined himself in. 'Well, let's just say it's all a bit disorganised. We can say they're on the French coast somewhere near the Belgian border.'

Mr Sellick examined the map. 'Right, so they'll be embarking from Boulogne, from Calais, possibly Dunkirk...'

Chrissie looked on in admiration, impressed by her father's grasp of strategy. Her uncle remained cautious. 'Um...just the last one, Wally.'

'What! You mean Dunkirk? Why not the other two?'

Uncle Stephen didn't answer.

'You're not telling me...you're surely not telling me the Boche have got Calais and Boulogne already? You can't mean that.'

No answer.

'Right then.' Mr Sellick slammed the old atlas shut in a puff of dust. 'End of story. Next stop Paris. After that, London.'

Uncle Stephen stood and leant his long body awkwardly against the mantelpiece. 'Let's keep it practical, if we can. The thing is, we need every boat we can get out there. Every single one will save lives, give Britain a better chance in future. They'll be operating from several ports. The destroyers, mine-sweepers and so on – the big stuff – they're going out from Dover, because the harbour's deep enough to take them. Some minesweepers and passengers ships will disembark troops at Margate. As for Ramsgate...we'll be sending out the little boats – hundreds of them, if we can find enough.'

Listening to her uncle, Chrissie got a glimpse of the capable administrator in action. Even so, she dared to interrupt him. 'Forgive me uncle, but I don't understand why little boats are needed. I mean one like ours will take a couple of dozen men at best. It doesn't make sense when you compare it to the capacity of a destroyer.'

'Actually Chrissie, destroyers are remarkably ill-equipped for transporting men. But you make a good point, and I'll try to answer it. And I insist once again that neither of you say a single word about this to anyone else.'

'Don't worry uncle,' she said, glad he hadn't bitten her head off. There were times when she almost liked him.

The clock on the mantelpiece struck the hour and her uncle made an anxious time check before continuing. 'Now then...Dunkirk harbour isn't designed to handle a big army like this one – more than three hundred thousand men, and that's without taking the French into account.'

'We're surely not bringing *them* back,' Mr Sellick burst out.

Uncle Stephen merely raised his eyebrows. 'Much of the harbour has been damaged, but there's some relatively deep water and there's a long containing wall – they call it a mole. Actually it wasn't built for embarkation purposes but it'll do at a pinch. Of course the Germans will try everything they can to prevent ships getting away. They're shelling from batteries nearby and the Luftwaffe are much in evidence. It's a real hot potato. The ships are pretty helpless while they're stationary at the mole. So...'

'So, we use the beaches,' said Mr Sellick.

'Well done, Wally – yes the beaches. We still have some eight miles of beaches under Allied control, stretching north-east from the harbour. And that's a much less frenetic scene. So the Dynamo strategy is to take men off from the mole *and* the beaches for as long as possible. There's just one problem.'

'The shelving,' said Mr Sellick.

'Right again. The Dunkirk beaches shelve very gradually. It's a nightmare, actually. No way you can get big ships anywhere near – it's enough of a challenge for a small motor yacht. So the destroyers and other bigger beasts lie off the coast, and the little boats take men from the beaches and ferry them out. Get the picture? And they need to do that over and over again till they run low on fuel and have to go back to Blighty. What's the draught on your boat, Wally?'

'Just over three feet,' said Mr Sellick.

'Hm. I have to admit that makes her very attractive to the Admiralty – for the beach work, you understand.'

'There's just one thing,' said Mr Sellick. 'How do your people match up the two elements? Enough men in the two locations – the harbour and the beach – to feed the ships, enough ships in place to take on the men?'

Uncle Stephen looked at his brother-in-law with new eyes. 'Maybe they ought to put you in charge of this operation, Wally. That's a very pertinent question.'

'Thank you, brother-in-law.' Mr Sellick bowed formally. 'We're surely not going to start getting on with each other after all this time, are we? And the answer is?'

'The answer is we *don't* match up the men with the boats.'

'*What!*'

'I mean we ought to, of course, but so far we've not found a way of doing it. I told you, communications are hopeless. There's no decent contact between Dover and the Expeditionary Force and none between the harbour and the beaches. So it's all pot luck for the poor devils on the ground.'

'Bloody hell, Stephen.'

Uncle Stephen spread his hands helplessly. 'I know. Look, I've come round to give you as much information as I dare. You're family, and I owe it to you. But if you were to think of going out there in your own boat, well...it's a horrible decision to make. You've seen Molly's reaction – she's barely speaking to me. I can't pretend this Dunkirk business will be anything but extremely dangerous. Some of the boat owners who go out there are going to die.'

'I get the picture,' said Mr Sellick.

'No Wally, I want you to hear. The area you'd be going to is a nightmare for navigation. Some of the most dangerous shoals in Europe, and they're not properly marked because a lot of the buoys have sunk. There are wrecks just below the water level and there'll be a lot more before this thing's finished. You'd be travelling at night without lights, in constant danger of being run down by passing destroyers, or overturned in their wash...'

'All right Stephen, I get it.'

'There's more. There are mines everywhere, including the magnetic mines, horrible things. Not so many U-boats in these shallow waters, but plenty of torpedo-boats instead. Then you've got the Luftwaffe and you've got shelling from the coastal batteries. And the troops on the beaches are desperate, you know – they've already overturned several small boats through lack of discipline.'

'That's enough dangers,' said Mr Sellick quietly.

Uncle Stephen actually smiled, a red-letter event. 'All right, I'll stop. But I am trying to put you off and I admit it. I owe that to Molly, and actually I think she's right. You don't have to go yourself, Wally. You can lease your boat to the Admiralty and they'll find naval people to handle it. That's what'll happen with most of the private craft that are not simply requisitioned. Molly's afraid you'll over-react because they wouldn't let you join up. In my opinion – for what it's worth – there's absolutely no need for you to feel that way.'

'It's not that.' Mr Sellick spoke dispassionately, and they both turned towards him. 'I think you know why I have to go.'

'Because of Tom.' It was Chrissie who spoke.

Mr Sellick nodded. 'Of course. We don't yet know what's happened to Tom...'

'And nor do I,' Uncle Stephen broke in. 'Please believe me when I say that.'

'He won't be in France, we know that now. But he might have been, just as easily. There'll be thousands of sons out there trying to get away, and thousands of families wanting them back. If you had children, Stephen...well, I'm sure you understand.'

Uncle Stephen put a hand on his brother-in-law's arm. 'All right, Wally. I can't argue on that one.'

'We *have* to go,' exclaimed Chrissie.

They both turned on her. 'Whoa, girl!' cried her father. 'There's no "we" about it.' He snorted. '*You're* not going.'

'Oh and why not, dad? You and me have taken *Blithe Spirit* out dozens of times. You know I can handle her. And I'm good with the motors, which is important in a long trip.'

'It's not that,' Uncle Stephen said. 'We know you're great with the boat, Chrissie. I've always admired you. Look, I've been closely involved all the way through, matching up crews and boats for Dynamo. There are hundreds of people involved – thousands, probably – and except for a few nurses on the hospital ships I don't know of a single woman amongst them. Please believe me.'

'Oh I believe you.' Chrissie spoke with passion, and it infuriated her that a drop of murky fluid – she didn't recognise tears – should choose this moment to spring from her right eye and roll down the cheek. 'Have you forgotten Tom's my brother? Forgive me, but you're slow to realise how things are changing in the world, you both are. Haven't you noticed what's happening in this war? Women are doing the jobs men have always done. They're in the armaments factories and driving the buses. They're signalling on the railways, they're smelting steel, and they're just as good as the men in most cases. They're working for the WAAF, learning the Morse Code to get into the Wrens. I'm a mechanic in a garage full of men, don't forget. You're turning a blind eye to half the population. Dammit, things are changing fast and the men need to change with them.'

'Well said, Chrissie,' was Mr Sellick's comment, 'But you're not going.'

Her father's reaction was no surprise but it infuriated her. Late that evening she left the house to walk off her frustration. Inevitably the route led down to the sea front. A policeman posted by the harbour gave her a suspicious glare but refrained from comment. It was dark, with low clouds masking the moon, but she could still make out a flotilla of five herring drifters nearing the harbour exit and she knew they'd be heading for France. She wanted to be on one of them, wishing with all her being to share whatever experiences they had to endure. She continued her walk, marching furiously along the length of the harbour before turning for home with resentment burning in her breast.

***   ***   ***

After Uncle Stephen's second visit events moved with surprising speed. On the morning of May 30ᵗʰ Mr Sellick went to see the 'Naval Officer in Charge, Ramsgate', who was operating from the harbour-master's hut. He was quickly passed on to a man called Malan, who seemed to know what he was doing despite being a new arrival in Ramsgate. He gave Malan a thumbnail sketch of his most cherished possession: a 30-foot motor yacht built by a Cornishman in 1925, two Ailsa Craig petrol engines driving two propellers. An hour later Mr Sellick extracted *Blithe Spirit* from her rickety boat-house and took her into harbour. It was a grey morning but his spirits soared to be back at the familiar tiller. He noted the motors' ready response after their 6-month lay-off, and gave silent thanks for Chrissie's attentions.

'Will she do?' he asked, as Malan looked over his boat for the first time.

'Oh she'll do Mr Sellick. You've kept her in excellent shape.' At this point Mr Sellick almost mentioned Chrissie's role, but something restrained him. 'To be perfectly honest,' Malan went on, 'We're sending across everything that will float at the moment.'

A glance round the harbour confirmed the truth of this remark. The place was a ferment of activity, more so than Mr Sellick could ever recall. Teams of Admiralty men had sprung up from nowhere, and under the direction of Malan and others like him were preparing craft of every description for their Channel crossings.

'I understand you're taking her over yourself,' Malan said.

'That's right.'

'And you can find another civilian to go with you?'

'Aye, the man who co-owns the boat. He's always wanted to do something like this.'

'And you can both get away? It's not easy for men in employment to drop everything, sign up to the Navy for a month.'

'I've already had a word with my guv'nor. Jim's self-employed, so that won't be a problem.'

'Good, that's a big help. We're having to spread a limited number of men across a lot of boats. What I can do is to let you have a naval rating to make up your crew to three. Young chap called Tyler. A good man. Strong on navigation, which can be a problem with weekend sailors. Many civilian skippers haven't been out of sight of land. Some don't even own a compass.'

He gave a searching look with the last comment and Mr Sellick reacted to it. 'We've got a compass, but I take your point. Much of our sailing's been along the coast. When are we likely to leave?'

'We've got a convoy going out tomorrow evening. That suit you?'

'Blimey. You're not wasting any time.'

Malan met his eye. 'Mr Sellick, I'm not allowed to tell you very much. To be honest I don't *know* very much. What we do know — all of us connected with this operation — is the need for urgency. Things are really bad out there. Yesterday is already too late. So are you up for it?'

'Don't you worry about that,' said Mr Sellick. 'You can count on us.'

Once he'd delivered *Blithe Spirit* into the Navy's hands Mr Sellick lost his control over her. He had less say than at any time in his seven years of ownership. He stood uselessly by as a working party prepared the little boat for the crossing. The men knew what they were doing all right, but they naturally lacked Mr Sellick's emotional attachment to her. Preparing for a full load of troops on the return, they stripped out the few items in the cabin that gave the boat a distinctive character — two cupboards, a cushioned seat, a box of clothing. They checked the motors and gave them a clean bill of health. They filled the water tanks and installed some additional containers because, as they explained, the scarcity of water in Dunkirk was at crisis level. They equipped the boat with considerably more ropes than she usually carried. Then they filled the fuel tanks.

'I can't believe this,' said Mr Sellick, as the precious petrol surged into his boat. 'This stuff would fetch a fortune on the black market.'

Malan grinned. 'One thing we can't do, I'm afraid, is to provide you with arms. We don't do that for any of the little boats. Maybe you wouldn't know what to do with a fire-arm anyway.'

'Maybe,' said Mr Sellick.

'There'll be a Lewis gun on the tug that's leading your convoy. That's the best we can manage. It's laid down as standard practice.'

Late that afternoon, as soon as he could get away, Mr Sellick called to see the man who was the co-owner of *Blithe Spirit*. He was looking forward to the visit because he knew it would give Jim a fillip to take an active part in the war effort. By the time he got home Chrissie had returned from work and his wife was once again fretting over the evening meal. They both looked up expectantly as he entered the dining room.

'So I suppose that's all sorted,' said Mrs Sellick. 'The pair of you have got your little *Boy's own* jaunt set up for tomorrow.'

'Not exactly,' he said.

'What's that supposed to mean?'

'I mean that Jim's not coming.'

In her surprise she chipped one of their best plates, banging it against the table. 'What! They won't have him?'

'They'd have him all right, but he doesn't want to come.'

Chrissie, seated at the table, was watching her father intently. She longed to speak but restrained herself. It was her mother who pressed on. '*Why* won't Jim do it?'

'He put up some tame excuses. I reckon he's scared.'

'Ha! I bet his wife's pleased.'

'She didn't look very pleased.'

Mrs Sellick went into the kitchen for a moment, but soon returned. 'Does that mean Jim won't let the boat make the trip?'

'Oh he's happy for it to be used. I think the Admiralty would take it anyway, whether Jim approved or not.'

He sat himself down at the table very deliberately and lit a cigarette. The atmosphere in the room was heavy with unspoken thoughts. Mrs Sellick stalked across to stand over her husband, hands on hips. 'Stop messing me about, Wally. What does this mean to us? Can this Malan person find a second man to make up the crew?'

'No, he can't. I've just been down there. That's why I'm so late. Without Jim I'd have to wait my turn. They're short of people.'

'So you're not going then. You've told him you can't go.'

'No Molly,' he said. 'I didn't do that.'

Chrissie rose from her seat without any apparent effort, as if she'd discovered the art of levitation, and gazed at her father with an expression of exaltation.

'That's right, Chrissie,' he said. 'I'd like you to come with me.'

'You know I will,' she said.

'So you'd better get rid of all that blond hair. The Admiralty men will stop the boat if they think I've got a woman on board.'

'Right dad, I'll do it now.'

'No, I'll do it,' said Mrs Sellick. She pushed Chrissie into the kitchen and sat her down and took the scissors from a drawer. Soon a little heap of blond locks had accumulated on the lino. Dinner was forgotten.

'Now if the worst happens you'll at least make a respectable corpse,' Mrs Sellick said.

'No Molly, *no*!' her husband remonstrated.

'That's fair, isn't it?' she said. 'If you must do this, go into it with your eyes open.'

While Chrissie for once sat meekly, Mrs Sellick seemed galvanised by events. Her scissor snipping had an almost manic quality. Throughout their married life Mr Sellick had never known what his wife would do next. He quite liked this aspect of their union though it left him at a disadvantage.

'We won't be away long,' he told her. 'Stephen will look in on you.'

'I'm not helpless,' she retorted. 'It's you and Chrissie need to look out for yourselves. Don't even blink, either of you.'

~ Three ~

Private Joseph Edwards felt scared. In sole charge of his truck on an empty road he was confused and lonely, but above all scared. He'd no idea where to go and little notion where he'd come from. He felt responsible for the vehicle and knew he must soon stop driving as darkness was descending. The Lower Somme landscape exacerbated his mood with its flat terrain dissected by ditches. The scarcity of trees meant little cover was accessible should he come under aerial attack.

Already it was almost dark. The bare countryside seemed menacing in the gloom, yet he refused to advertise his existence by using the vehicle's lights. Then just as driving was becoming impossible some straggling trees loomed up against the sky. He took his truck off the road and cautiously traversed the rough ground towards the overhanging foliage. He switched off the engine and stuck his head through the window to listen. The only sound was of leaves shifting in the breeze.

Joseph was hungry. He decided to eat something before the light gave out altogether, and arranged his rifle on the adjacent passenger seat, more to give the illusion of security than because he trusted himself to use it. He took a swig from his meagre supply of water, then poured more water into an old tin containing some of the army's uneatable biscuits. When they'd softened – a relative term – Joseph scraped some bully beef on top and forced the mixture down. Finally he wriggled into his great-coat and lay down across the front seats.

Sleep didn't come readily. Once Joseph heard a noise and raised his head to the level of the window. There was nothing but the dark mass of branches. Again he tried to settle down. It was hard not to dwell upon a situation that struck him as ominous – himself, alone, in a foreign country. Until recently he'd not been outside England.

The 2nd/5th Leicestershire were a territorial battalion who'd been sent to France for construction work. They'd only been in the country six weeks. Not for them the months of gentle induction into the phony war – the drinking in cafés, fraternising with the locals, getting the hang of a foreign location. They'd barely had time to know each other, let alone the crucial military details that enhanced the chances of survival in battle. The entire Expeditionary Force was under-prepared – according to an indiscreet conversation he'd overheard in the mess – but his own battalion was something else. They hadn't a clue. They had no idea how to handle night fighting, or to set the sights on their rifles, or to judge which of the shells that rained down on them were likely to be dangerous. They were a bunch of innocents consigned to slaughter.

The battalion had barely been six weeks in France when it was deployed to relieve the 2nd Essex at a place called Pont-a-Vendin. They were on the Deule canal, protecting a 4-mile section of the British front. An officer announced they'd be up against the German 12th Infantry Division, which signified nothing to Joseph but to anyone in the know meant their outfit never stood an earthly. Everything about that encounter was a surprise to them. When the action began Joseph thought the septic atmosphere meant the Leicesters were being gassed, till someone explained it was the stench of cordite from bursting shells. Some of the men had half-believed the rumours that German tanks were made from cardboard; as the first panzer unit showed up they were petrified by its speed and power, and there were several incidents of soldiers soiling themselves.

Despite all that Joseph reckoned the Leicesters had done OK. They were inept but hadn't lacked courage. They held their own for two days and a night before the Germans' superior power overwhelmed them. He tried not to dwell on the images that surfaced from those last hours; the bodies of men who'd barely been acquaintances but who'd eaten meals together and shared silly jokes to hide their fear. The dwindling band of survivors thought their last hour had come. When it was clear nothing more could be expected of them they were told to retreat towards the French coast, taking as many wounded as possible. In the confusion Joseph had no conception of how many men were left. The battalion split into fragments, his group comprising no more than 60 men.

At this point Joseph's military career suffered another downer. An officer told him to take one of the unit's trucks and 'forage for food' in the surrounding countryside. The order couldn't be disobeyed but he knew himself to be unsuited to the task. He at least had experience of driving a large vehicle – which was why he got chosen – but he spoke no word of the language and lacked the kind of brazen personality that could extort provisions from reluctant villagers. Worse, when he returned to the rendez-vous after four hours of fruitless searching, his unit had disappeared. There were few signs that 60 men, with all their equipment and possessions, had been present at all. It was this which led to his aimless driving around for the rest of the afternoon till darkness forced him off the road.

The following morning he woke after 9am in a more positive frame of mind. Surely if he set out for the coast he'd sooner or later come across more British units, and as a man in possession of a truck would be a popular acquisition for any company? But that wasn't how things turned out.   More people were on the roads, but none of them were British army. As far as he could tell they were refugees. There was no pattern to the way they straggled along the country lanes. At times there'd be one or two families in isolation, at others a long sequence of displaced people on both sides of the highway. A sprinkling of bikes showed amongst those on foot. Quite a lot of the women had a red blanket rolled up and worn diagonally over their shoulders and a beret on their heads, as if they were chorus members in an amateur musical. Others projected a poignant image, having left home in their best clothes.

Some of the pedestrians gesticulated as Joseph passed, obviously wanting lifts, but he hardened his heart and pressed on. The army had expressly forbidden them to pick up refugees on the road. He wondered why so many people *were* on the move. There was no question of Germans being active in this vicinity; they were miles away, restrained by British and French troops operating under a joint command.

Still a rank amateur in military matters, Joseph took too long to realise what was about to happen next. He'd just passed a field containing several cows with grossly swollen udders and was pondering what might have caused the phenomenon. There was no particular reason for noticing another posse of refugees a hundred yards ahead except that, belatedly, he saw three Stuka planes bearing down on them. Out of nowhere came a tremendous crash, and that stretch of ground disintegrated, earth and debris flying 30 feet into the air. More mayhem followed as a secondary wave of incendiary bombs laid waste to the surrounding area. Before the dust settled Joseph had realised the delicacy of his own position, sitting as he was behind the wheel of a British army truck in broad daylight. He braked and wrenched the vehicle so abruptly off the road that it scraped along yards of fencing, uprooting several posts. As soon as it was stationary he grabbed his great-coat, threw open the door and leapt into the road, then ran hell-for-leather across a meadow to dive behind a hedge.

He lay gasping for breathe as the Stukas passed overhead. At first relieved to see them go, he recoiled when the trio turned in a broad loop and headed back. As Joseph watched, the leading plane peeled away from the others and dived towards the truck, making a hellish screaming unlike anything he'd heard before. Because he'd ducked down, bringing both arms above his head in a futile gesture of self-protection, he didn't see his truck jump into the air and shudder down again. A mass of black smoke drifted away across the still peaceful fields. Even then it wasn't over, because another Stuka dived over the scene of the first explosion; Joseph heard the machine gun rat-tat-tat and saw the refugee bodies twitch as bullets disturbed them.

'Don't move,' came a voice from nearby on his right.

Instinctively disregarding the instruction he turned to make out someone's head and shoulders concealed in the undergrowth. From the man's uniform and the nasal twang of his speech he decided this was, astonishingly, an English soldier. He could make out the corporal's stripes on his sleeve.

'Don't move,' the voice repeated, more urgently, 'Or we'll be next.'

'All right, I won't.' This time Joseph was more careful. 'But why did they do that?' he cried out. 'Why machine-gun helpless civilians?'

'They're Germans,' the voice explained. 'They enjoy it.'

'And that ghastly noise. What *was* that?'

'You new around here then?'

'Well I've seen these planes in the distance, but nothing so...ugh! what a horrible sound!'

'The Stukas have sirens attached. Typical Boche wheeze. Fucking savages. You get used to it.'

'I hope I don't have to.'

'We can make a move now,' said the man, climbing to his feet as the German aircraft disappeared over the horizon. The newcomer was a little chap, five foot four at most. His swarthy face had thick lips and a knowing expression and he spoke in an offhand, querulous sort of way, so that Joseph couldn't decide whether the man was a habitual backslider or just didn't give a damn.

'I'm Arthur,' the bloke said.

'Joseph.'

They shook hands, as if they'd been introduced at a dinner-dance event.

'Joseph, crikey. Was your old man religious, then?'

'Well...I don't know if it was that. But yes, we're Methodists.'

'I'll 'ave to mind me Ps and Qs then.' The man cocked his head to subject Joseph to scrutiny. 'So what were you doing bowling along down there? Out for an afternoon spin?'

Joseph explained about the action at Pont-a-Vendin and being separated from his battalion. 'There aren't very many of us left. We were never supposed to fight. I'm an engineer, not a soldier.'

'A respectable occupation,' said Arthur. 'I'm a Don R.'

'A what-er?'

'You *are* green behind the ears. It's army slang for despatch rider.'

'Is that right. But wouldn't a despatch rider have a motorbike?'

By way of response Arthur inclined his head towards the undergrowth ten yards distant. Joseph just about caught the glint of sun on a metal part. Arthur moved to heave the bike upright and gestured towards the blackened remains of the truck, still burning noisily at the side of the road.

'I know engineers can fix anything, but that one might be a job and a half. So do you want a lift?'

'That's good of you. It'd be better than walking. But shouldn't we go and check on those refugees?'

Arthur shook his head. 'No point. We ain't got nothing to offer 'em. The trick out here is to keep moving. You coming?'

Joseph hesitated.

'You're going to have to get used to this, you know. War's a miserable business. We'll report it to a Froggy first-aid post – that's if we see one. If the buggers ever get their act together.'

'All right then.' Joseph knew the man was right, but every instinct urged him to approach the line of bodies at the roadside. He knew he'd be thinking about them for days to come. He shrugged himself into the great-coat, feeling – a stroke of good fortune this – the reassuring shape of his water bottle in one of the pockets. 'Are you sure you can take a passenger?'

'God yes. Don't worry about that. They're not built for two but it happens all the time. Specially with junior officers, when the poor devils can't get into staff cars. Come on then.' Arthur patted his bike with the sort of affection most men would have shown to a dog. 'This is my little helpmate.'

'BSA M20,' said Joseph.

Arthur looked up, surprised. 'You into bikes, then?'

'I'm an engineer, remember.'

'Then climb on, my friend.' Arthur started the machine and revved up, driving slowly and as quietly as possible past the recumbent bodies. It occurred to Joseph that his companion felt no better than he did about leaving in such circumstances. There was no movement at all from the pathetic figures on the verge.

They'd both squeezed onto the BSA all right and it helped that Joseph had been on motorbikes before. The only tricky bit was where to put his feet. He'd noticed straight away that Arthur was constantly peering around at the sky. After a couple of miles the man suddenly pulled the bike into a copse at the roadside. He killed the engine and reiterated his mantra about 'not moving'.

'What's up?' Joseph asked.

'Messerschmidt.'

'Oh. I didn't see him. He wouldn't bother with one bike, surely?'

'Are you kidding! They've gotta have their fun.' He patted the BSA playfully. 'It's all right, girl. We'll be off in a tick.'

'You seem very fond of her,' observed Joseph.

'She's a darling. Aren't you a fan?'

'Well, you know. Plenty of other possibilities. Ariels, Triumphs. The Matchless G3L.'

'Of course – the eternal daydream,' cried Arthur in exasperation. 'Always the Matchless.'

'Well it's a good machine. Don't you think so?'

'D'you know how many BSAs have had to be made for the war? Well I don't either but it must be tens of thousands.' Now the Messerschmidt had gone he swung a leg over to stand beside his machine, and Joseph followed suit. 'Look, the BSA's a low tech job and it's made from cast iron. *No aluminium.*' He patted his bike again. 'You must know about the aluminium shortage.'

'Goodness yes,' acknowledged Joseph. 'My mum's handed in most of her saucepans so they can make fighter planes.'

'That's just it. I wouldn't have a bike at all if they only made the Matchless. No, the BSA suits me fine. Of course I got one of the REME fitters to customize mine. They'll always do it for a packet of fags.'

'What speed can you do?'

'Ah well now. It'll go up to 60 but that's not a good idea. Forty miles an hour – you can keep that up all day.'

'And petrol consumption?'

'The tank takes three gallons and it'll do 50 miles a gallon. Takes any old stuff too. Reckon I could run it on lemonade.' He stopped and laughed, at himself as much as anything. 'You know, this sort of conversation can only happen when there's an engineer present. We could be a good team, you and me.' He got back on the BSA. 'Come on, let's get going.'

'Arthur, where exactly are we making for?'

His companion turned in the saddle. 'That's difficult to say. I don't have any more messages to deliver. I should be trying to join my unit, but where the hell are they? So I think the answer to your question is –

away from the Germans, wherever they might be.'

Less than 20 minutes later their road crossed a major highway. Joseph was astonished to see some British troops running down it in what struck him as a highly undisciplined fashion. He was further surprised to see a sergeant from the Royal Military Police directing people, with another member of the force in a slit trench nearby.

'What's up mate?' said Arthur, drawing alongside the sergeant.

'Haven't you heard? Krauts have broken through.'

'Get away.' Arthur exchanged an "amazed" look with his passenger. 'So where are they now?'

'How long is a piece of string,' said the sergeant. 'They're to the south and they're to the east. More than that I can't say. My advice is keep north-west towards the coast until one of our esteemed leaders decides what to do next. And I'd go the long way round, seeing as how you've got wheels.' He indicated the minor road straight ahead. 'The main highway's more direct but it's a bit too exposed.'

Soon afterwards the bike was bowling along the designated road at Arthur's standard '40 miles an hour' when they heard the sudden roar of aeroplane engines. A machine gun let rip and divots flew up from the bitumen to their right.

Arthur cursed and swung violently the other way. 'Hold on tight. Bastards have crept up behind us. They do that.'

For several minutes Joseph saw a manifestation of what Arthur had described earlier – a Messerschmidt pilot 'having his fun'. The BSA whirled crazily about the road as though its rider had breakfasted on double whiskies. The pilot in his turn dived from any number of vantage points; from ahead, behind and both sides. Joseph was in a cold sweat whenever the plane stayed behind them, expecting bullets to rake his neck and back. But Arthur had clearly done this before and managed to keep them out of trouble. There was a rehearsal of an unhappy ending as the bike passed a field of crops, and Joseph saw a line of corn heads neatly sheared from their stalks a yard away. At last – oh welcome sight! – a dense belt of trees surged into view on their right. Arthur left the road and, still zigzagging, took them across a patch of rough ground to ease under the protective cover of branches. He turned off the engine and they heard the Messerschmidt roar away. Joseph felt a sense of soothing peace under their silent canopy.

'Phew,' he said, more shaken up than he cared to let on.

'Piece of cake,' said Arthur in his querulous drawl.

After a moment Joseph started to look around. He exclaimed loudly and nudged his companion, indicating that they were not the only British soldiers to shelter under these trees.

'Blimey,' said Arthur.

At first they saw just a couple of men in uniforms, then several more, then behind them what looked like the outline of a staff car, and quite possibly another staff car beyond that. Before they could investigate one of the men walked towards them. It was clear from his confident manner, let alone the three pips on his shoulder, that this was an officer – a captain, no less.

'Hello there.' The man sketched a willowy response to their salutes. 'Hardy's my name. For a moment there we were afraid you'd given away our hiding place.'

'Didn't know you were here, sir,' said Joseph.

'Oh that's all right. No damage done. Making for anywhere in particular?'

'We wish we knew,' Arthur chipped in. 'We've both got separated from our units.'

'Join the club. There are British troops wandering about all over the area. We're hoping to introduce some order before long.'

No sooner had Joseph absorbed the magisterial 'we' in this response than Arthur, staring into the wood, did a double-take.

'Blow me down...' He recovered himself and tried to inject respect into a voice that wasn't designed for respect. 'Sorry sir, but I thought I saw...that man behind the car, sir...he's the spitting image...'

'Quite right,' said Hardy. 'You've got good eyes, corporal. That is indeed our leader.'

'It's just that he's hard to miss, sir,' Arthur went on.

'Oh I know. Great bear of a man, isn't he.'

'It's General Gort,' Arthur advised his companion, in response to an enquiring glance.

'Who?'

'You'll have to forgive him, sir,' Arthur told the captain. 'He's with the Territorials. Only been in the country six weeks.'

'It's perfectly all right,' Hardy reassured Joseph. 'For the record, Lord Gort's the commanding officer of the Expeditionary Force. Now look, you chaps, there's no need for us to stand on ceremony in these circumstances.' Hardy sat himself down on a fallen tree trunk and motioned the others to follow suit. Not that they had any choice, but already they felt content to oblige the man. He had the accent of the officer class without the toffee-nosed manner that so often affronted other ranks. 'Our party's just stopped here for a spot of lunch,' he went on. 'We're on our way to set up a new HQ – I'd better not say where, exactly. Now if I can offer you two a bit of advice...'

'We need it, sir,' said Arthur. 'We don't know where to make for.'

'Exactly.' Hardy thought for a moment. 'This is a bit tricky. You'll see why when I tell you. It's like this. General Gort has already determined his strategy for the Expeditionary Force. Only thing is, he hasn't exactly passed it up the chain, because they want us to do something else. When I say "up the chain" I'm talking about Churchill and Co.'

The pair exchanged a baffled glance. Hardy raised his eyebrows towards Joseph. 'I expect you've heard of Winston Churchill.'

'I'm sorry about that, sir,' said Joseph.

'It's all right – only pulling your leg. So...I'll tell you where to make for, and you can even pass the information on – in fact I hope you do, only don't say where you got it from. Not for a couple of days anyway.'

They both stared at him.

'So my advice to you two – make that an order – is to head for the port of Dunkirk.'

'Dunkirk, sir!' exclaimed Arthur.

'That's right. Not Boulogne and certainly not Calais, but Dunkirk. There'll be ships lifting troops from Dunkirk and taking them back home. The sooner you get there, the quicker you'll get away.'

'I'm sorry sir,' Arthur began. 'I don't really get it. I mean if the nobs in Blighty...'

'I know, I know – you've got a dozen questions in your head, but you'll understand I can't answer most of them. Shouldn't have told you really. I'll just say two things about strategy. General Gort is the man on the ground, and that's always key. And secondly, this is about leadership.' He gazed rather fondly to where Gort and company were standing around quaffing glasses of wine. 'It's about making the right decision – the only decision, actually – and to hell with popularity and personal advancement. Now then...'

He stood, and the other two jumped up with him. 'Who exactly am I addressing here?'

They told him their names. Most unusually – for this was the British army – Hardy stepped forward and shook their hands rather than saluting. 'Very good luck to both of you.'

***   ***   ***

They made reasonable progress during the afternoon, though Arthur pulled off the road twice more as German fighter planes materialised overhead. He was starting to worry about fuel, and kept their speed constant at the 40mph mark. They saw more batches of refugees but – to their relief – no repeat of the morning's bloodbath; better still, no sign of the German troops that were said to have 'broken through'. With the peaceful French countryside all around, it could be hard to believe a war was in progress at all.

As the light started to fail Arthur took his bike off the road again. He pointed to a farmhouse and barn some two hundred yards distant. 'When the word about Dunkirk gets out it'll be more and more difficult to find billets. Impossible as we near the port. Blokes'll be sleeping in ditches and empty sewage pipes – all sorts – anywhere to keep out of sight.'

'But today...?' Joseph prompted.

'Let's check out the farmhouse. The country folk have been quite friendly so far. They'll let us sleep in their barn as long as there are no Germans about.' He revved up briefly. 'Come on, let's try our luck. Keep an eye open for Kraut transports.'

He took the bike along a rough track to the farmhouse. When they got closer a pungent, pig-like aroma assailed them. A barking dog ran alongside, but seemed friendly enough. There was no sign of the Germans.

As they arrived, the farmhouse door opened and a young woman appeared on the step. Using sign language she urged them to park round the corner of the building, then to come back into the house. Joseph thought he understood her concern about security. If there was to be any fraternising – with British or German soldiers – she wanted it to stay out of sight.

Inside, the girl led them into the kitchen. The room was warm from a lit stove and spectacularly untidy, with foodstuffs littered all over the place. Two cats snoozed under the table. An old woman was slumped in a cane chair from which she could only have emerged with difficulty. There were no men around, which was not unusual in wartime.

Arthur embarked upon a routine of sign language, interspersed with about three words that resembled French. He was addicted to the term 'peut-etre', which he later described as 'a valuable all-purpose item of vocabulary'. For instance he would point towards the barn, make a 'sleeping' gesture with both hands under his chin, then throw in a 'peut-etre' with a questioning inflection. There was also communication about food, with Arthur brandishing a note of the local currency. It all seemed to end satisfactorily, with cash changing hands and smiles on both sides. Joseph felt fortunate to have fallen in with his Don R friend, who'd managed to develop such wheeler-dealer skills in his short life.

A few minutes later the two men were together in the barn. This turned out to be exactly how Joseph – an inveterate city-dweller – had imagined a barn would look: a single door, no windows but a crude skylight in the roof, bales of hay piled high along one side, several chickens running about a concrete floor. It was pleasantly warm.

'The upshot of all that haggling,' said Arthur, 'Is we can stay the night. The girl's going to bring us some hot grub a couple of hours from now. We're not allowed to smoke inside though. I had to promise.'

'Quite right,' said Joseph. 'She doesn't want all this hay going up in flames.'

'I'll tell you what she does want.' Arthur kicked absent-mindedly at a passing chicken.

'What d'you mean?'

'Don't tell me you didn't notice.'

'What? Notice what?'

Arthur rolled his eyes, a just visible gesture in the gathering darkness. 'You didn't see her looking? That's what women do when they fancy a bloke. You really didn't notice?'

Joseph felt his cheeks going red. 'Don't talk daft.' He'd not noticed anything of the kind.

'Hm! She'll be round here given half a chance, soon as I leave you alone. You see. Bet you ten francs.'

'This is ridiculous. I don't go in for betting.'

'Course not, you're a Methodist. And I bet that's something else you don't go in for, eh?' He jogged Joseph's shoulder with an elbow. 'You know, the old how's yer father? You don't, do you?'

'If you're referring to...'

'Yes pardner, I do mean that.'

'I haven't so far, if you really want to know. Methodists believe in keeping that sort of thing for marriage. Anyway, give a thought to her circumstances. That poor girl has probably got a husband away in the war.'

'I'm just telling you what I saw.'

'If you're so sure she's...you know...you do it. I'll make myself scarce.'

'Don't worry, I would if I thought there was half a chance, but it doesn't work that way. Once a woman's made up her mind – a process beyond all understanding, by the way – nothing can change it. You'll learn.' He started marching furiously up and down the limited space, scattering chickens in his wake. 'Bloody hell, what a waste! I'm going outside. I'll feel better when I've had a fag. And I'll scout out the road while I'm about it – make sure the Boche aren't around.'

After he'd left, Joseph lay back against a bale of hay. The barn was peaceful, with only the odd cluck or flutter of wings disturbing the silence. The gloom was redeemed by a tranquil glow from the moon, penetrating the skylight. He felt at peace with himself, more so than since the day the Territorials had boarded their ship at Dover six weeks earlier.

He wasn't aware that his eyes had closed, but suddenly the girl was gliding across the barn's concrete floor like a ghost, illuminated by an oil lamp held in one hand. Joseph was embarrassed and scrambled to his feet. She kept moving till her slender form was inches away from his. The sound of her breathing seemed to fill the place. She must have put on perfume because he felt almost dizzy from the powerful scent of her.

Afterwards when Arthur pestered him for details, Joseph really couldn't bring them to mind. Part of him was deeply ashamed of the encounter. At the same time he longed to revisit it, to savour every second of the overwhelming experience. He remembered lying back on the hay with the girl above him, and the steady motion of her bare waist against his hand. He had an image of her parted lips in the cinematic lighting of the lamp. Perhaps he'd made some sort of noise, but couldn't be sure. It was *her* cry that stayed with him, like no sound he'd ever imagined. He knew he'd remember it for the rest of his life.

They must have held each other afterwards but again the scene had gone from his whirling brain. He only knew the girl had pointed to her breast and whispered one word.

'Therese'.

And he'd put a hand against his own chest.

'Joseph.'

And she'd quaintly reiterated his name under her breath.

After that he could only recall her slight form flitting back to the door, lamp in hand, a memory as detached as if she were a celluloid projection, with himself watching from a back seat in his local flea-pit. She left the barn without looking back.

When she'd gone the last person he wanted to confront was Arthur, but all too soon his mate came bouncing back bushy-tailed, bringing a whiff of nicotine in his wake.

'Blimey O'Reilly,' were his first words. 'So...you believe in keeping it for marriage. You must have meant *her* marriage.'

'I'm sorry, Arthur.' Joseph lolled back feeling awful and wonderful at one and the same time. 'I've behaved like a complete louse. I didn't mean to, honestly.'

Arthur patted him on the shoulder. 'Don't take it too hard, mate. Strange things happen in wartime. I just hope it doesn't delay the grub – I'm starving.' He contemplated the limp figure sprawled before him. 'You know, it's a good job you're a Methodist and not a Catholic. You could have had a field day with the guilt on this one.'

Joseph was barely listening. 'Suppose I've made her pregnant,' he brooded, mostly to himself.

'No, no, no – that's not a problem.' Arthur was in his most ebullient mood. 'You're Joseph, don't forget.'

'What are you talking about?'

'Don't you see – if she had one up the spout from you, her Froggy mates would know it was an immaculate conception.'

Joseph had a sense of humour, but it kicked in more slowly than most people's. He gave a belated snort, then reined himself in, thinking of what his father would say. He sat up and started a vigorous rubbing of his head, as if to clear it. An uncle had told him war would broaden his mind, but Joseph was finding himself unequal to its complexities.

'Do you want the good news?' Arthur said. 'No sign at all of the Krauts. The only movement out there is in the pig sty. I won't go into details. And you know what?'

'What now?'

'After this little incident I'm going to give you a name change. You can't be a Joseph, romping round Froggyland like Casanova. You're going to be "Jos". That's your new name. Don't worry, it'll suit you.'

*** *** ***

The next morning the pair were on their way again. They called at the farmhouse to thank the girl, and this time Joseph did see her looking. He did plenty of looking himself, more than he'd ever done in his life. But the imperative to move on couldn't be denied. 'Come on, mate,' murmured Arthur, taking his companion's arm to lever him from the shambolic kitchen. The last thing Joseph saw was the girl's unfathomable expression as she stood frozen at the kitchen table. He walked out to the bike like a zombie.

There were more British troops on the roads now, and the numbers swelled as Arthur and Joseph threaded their way north-west. Most laboured on foot, and the two men felt increasingly fortunate to have the bike. What struck Joseph about the retreat – people had started to call it that – was its anarchic character. Like themselves so many men had become detached from their regiments and pushed on in disorderly fashion with no clear destination. When they passed on Captain Hardy's information about Dunkirk the usual response was one of surprise.

Troops and refugees were often found in the same locations, albeit moving in different directions. The latter – on the rare occasions there was a common language for communication – were dismayed that the British had disengaged from the enemy. They were a dispiriting sight, overburdened on the road with mounds of household goods. At least soldiers had only their rifles to care for.

Arthur became preoccupied with finding petrol for the bike. He stopped several times at vehicles abandoned by the roadside and eventually had some joy. Out came a length of rubber tubing from his saddlebag, and a gallon of the precious fuel was transferred to the BSA. This piece of luck sparked a resumption of the little chap's infuriating whistling.

As the two moved on, talking *en route* with foot-sloggers from various units, a new picture began to emerge. Suddenly the buzz on everyone's lips was the word 'corridor'. 'What d'you mean, corridor?' said an irritated Arthur to a big sergeant, 'What is this sodding corridor we keep hearing about?' The sergeant's information was a lot more precise than their own hazy references to Dunkirk. It seemed the Allies had concentrated their remaining forces to protect a so-called 'corridor' for retreating troops. It ran through towns like Hazebrouck, Cassel and Bergues right through to Dunkirk port, with French and British regiments detailed to protect strategic points along the way. Those units were the unlucky ones, because they'd be the last to leave, if they left at all. All the other forces – the defeated and dispersed men straggling through the French countryside – had only to reach Dunkirk under their own steam. What they'd find when they got there – well, that was a subject on which nobody had reliable information.

Clearly there'd been ferocious engagements with the Germans in the area, yet by chance Joseph and Arthur avoided them. Occasionally they saw evidence of an action and wished they hadn't. Once they passed through a village laid waste by conflict, and Arthur had drawn up outside an old barn.

'I'll wait here Jos,' he'd said. 'Stick your head inside – see if it'd be a good place to get off the road. We could scout round for some grub.'

The barn door was half open and Joseph approached with care. There was little enough light inside, but it was sufficient for him to recoil instinctively. A score of wounded British soldiers were spilled across the dirt floor as two doctors tried to treat them by candlelight. The wounds were horrific and Joseph couldn't imagine men leaving this slaughter-house alive. The place reeked of blood. There was an unsettling silence save for the odd coughing fit or searing groan. He withdrew and returned to the bike shaking his head, unable to speak. They rode on.

They passed a signpost to Hazebrouck, but the pall of black smoke above the town deterred them from investigating; the British experience in France had suggested that any serious action ended with Germans in control. Five miles north-west lay Cassel, and here the evidence was more ambiguous. In a ravaged landscape were abandoned panzer tanks and other vehicles, some burnt out, others still blazing. The town itself stood 500 feet above, served by a steep road zig-zagging up the hillside. By now they badly needed more food, but the risk of exploring Cassel seemed too great. Besides, rain had started to come down. They left the forlorn scene, and its savage hissing sound as rainfall descended on the burning tanks.

The next village – they never did get the name – came upon them so suddenly there was no question of checking for Germans. That the buggers *had* been there was soon confirmed beyond dispute. Arthur took the bike under trees to one side of the village centre. He killed the engine and sat watching, on the alert for trouble. The small central square presented a picture of utter devastation. Debris was strewn everywhere, with the bodies of two civilians lying amongst it. Few of the surrounding buildings had been left undamaged, and there was the familiar sight of burnt-out vehicles, which by now left them unmoved.

The natural landscape had suffered too. Tree tops were sheared clean away and a tree-trunk had crashed onto an ornamental seat where villagers would have sat around in fine weather. A telegraph pole was another casualty, and a live wire crackled as the breeze stirred it against the ground.

'Keep well clear of that,' said Arthur. He pointed to a corner, where the village shop had once been situated. 'Let's have a shufti. I think we're in the clear.'

They wheeled the bike across, rather than restarting the engine and creating a din. The place looked distinctly unpromising. The front window had been smashed to smithereens, exposing empty shelves beyond. The ground in front was littered with rubbish.

Joseph was stunned by the scene of desolation. 'It brings it home seeing all this in one small village,' he said. 'What a dreadful, horrible waste.'

Arthur shushed him and drew his pistol. They got access to the shop by stepping through the window frame. Its shelves had been comprehensively looted. No food of any kind had survived save for a packet of dog biscuits which Arthur pocketed.

'Perhaps it'll come to that,' he said. He gazed across the village centre. 'We'll have to try one of the cottages. I never like doing it but needs must.'

They traversed the square, still wheeling the bike, and stopped at a cottage that was relatively unscathed. The front door opened when Arthur tried the handle.

'People do that,' he observed. 'Leave the door unlocked so it doesn't get broken down by strangers.'

They went cautiously inside. Joseph had never entered someone's home uninvited and felt acutely uncomfortable. He wondered whether a thief would feel the same, going about his nocturnal activities.

'I don't like this at all,' he said.

'I know,' Arthur admitted. 'But we're not going to damage the place, are we?'

The first thing they saw was a birdcage suspended from the ceiling. A canary lay dead on the lining of the base. Arthur tutted.

They were in a sort of dining room attached to the kitchen. A closed door led to the only other room downstairs. A scrabbling noise came from within. They looked at each other.

'Better open it,' said Arthur.

There was no need for the pistol Arthur waved around when they threw the door open, because the sole occupant of the room was a dog. Released from captivity it dashed round the living area barking dementedly. It was impossible to say how long the creature had been shut up there but the room itself was in a state, with ordure all down one side and various empty dishes that had presumably contained food. A strong smell of urine prevailed. The dog was surprisingly clean. It resembled an old English sheepdog crossed with some dodgier breed. The animal had an alert expression and was immediately friendly to the new arrivals, not blaming them for its incarceration.

Arthur took the dog biscuits from his pocket and scattered some on the floor. The creature demolished them in an instant, then jumped up to lick his hand.

'Friend for life,' said Joseph.

'I like dogs,' Arthur said. 'What shall we call him?'

'We won't know him long enough to need a name.'

'Everyone must have a name. I'm Arthur, you're Jos...'

'I'm *not* Jos.'

'He's Jos all right,' Arthur told the dog. 'And as for you, my shaggy friend, what are you called?'

'Well we found him locked up,' Joseph pointed out, 'So...maybe Jailbird?'

'Mm, I see where you're going with this.'

'All right then – if you don't like Jailbird, what about Old Lag?'

'That's it – Lag.' Arthur stooped to ruffle the dog's ears. 'Yes, Lag. Yes you, Lag. Definitely. See – he knows.' He straightened up. 'Let's see what else we can find.'

They went out of the back door into the garden. There was a small shed containing an ancient lawnmower and a woman's bicycle. Back in the house the dog started scratching at a closed door.

'What's that about?' said Arthur. He clapped a hand to his forehead. 'I tell you what. A lot of French peasants cure meat in their basement. A ham, or whatever. Perhaps Lag's onto something. Worth a look, anyway.'

They descended some steps into an evil-smelling cellar. They had just enough light to reveal that there was indeed a large ham dangling from a hook in the wall. The dog went berserk trying to reach it. Arthur lifted the meat from its place.

'God Jos, we're going to have a proper lunch for once.'

'I'll knock something together,' said Joseph. 'You have a rest. You deserve one.'

Out of the cellar again, they investigated the rest of the cottage. It was a curious experience poking their noses into the life of a family they were never going to meet. The building seemed to be occupied solely by adults, perhaps an elderly couple. No sign of children, present or past; no children's toys, or even photographs of children. A sacred picture in the main bedroom suggested devout Catholicism. In the kitchen Joseph opened a cupboard and found a small hoard of foodstuffs: some potatoes, a few onions (just about worth cooking) and a tin of carrots. A package wrapped in greaseproof paper disclosed cheese that was too far gone for even their desperate palates.

He felt uncomfortable about taking these pathetic offerings, but knew they'd soon be spoilt beyond anyone's use. For a short while the owners of this lowly dwelling tugged at his conscience. Who were they? Where were they now?: on the road somewhere, subjected – as he knew well enough – to lethal fire from German fighter planes?; with friends or relatives in another town? But then was any home safe from the panzer units that were trashing everything in sight?

An hour later the kitchen harboured the aroma of cooked meat and the pair sat down to the best meal either of them had enjoyed for weeks. It tasted all the better given that nothing like it would be coming their way in the near future. They gave Lag more of the dog biscuits and a few slices of ham but – as Arthur insisted – 'Not too many or he'll have the mother of all belly aches'.

Afterwards they sat back with their own bellies full, all too aware that they had to hit the road again. The sooner you get to Dunkirk the quicker you'll get away, Captain Hardy had told them. They topped up their water bottles and stuffed Arthur's saddle-bag with the remnants of food from the larder. Arthur put the ham back where he'd found it, just in case the occupants returned. They hadn't the heart to lock Lag up again, so left him running free in the cottage with the back door open into the garden. All too soon they found themselves standing beside the BSA in the village square. As before the place was deserted. With the exception of Lag they'd not seen a single living creature since arriving.

Arthur was looking around morosely, unlike his usual chirpy self. 'I don't like this,' he grumbled. 'I've got one of my feelings.'

'What d'you mean? What's wrong?'

'Can't tell you that. I just know. When I get one of my feelings it's best to look out.'

'It's a pity you didn't get one before you came to France in the first place,' said Joseph, trying to jolly him out of it. 'This isn't like you. You're the one who cheers *me* up. You're the cheeky chappie. You're the tuneless whistler.'

'I'm not happy,' said Arthur.

But as there was nothing else to do, they mounted the bike and started the motor.

~ Four ~

With 24 hours' grace before they set off for France, Mr Sellick and
Chrissie had their hands full. She needed to explain her absence to the
garage without giving the real reason or saying how long she'd be gone.
She fell back on lying, which she could manage convincingly when it was
in a good cause. A cock-and-bull story about first aid courses for the Red
Cross satisfied her boss. It was an era when just about anything was
acceptable if you mentioned 'the war effort'.

Chrissie spent a while checking her appearance in Mrs Sellick's
bedroom mirror. She'd never had to pass for a bloke before and it taxed
her powers of imagination. Her blond hair – what remained of it – was
concealed easily enough under a woolly hat, and her usual boating
clothes passed muster except in one respect. She tried binding her
breasts in the manner of actresses playing male roles, but it felt
uncomfortable as hell. Eventually she settled for an old, very loose
sweater of her father's with a jacket over the top. She didn't *feel*
feminine under that lot and hoped she didn't look it either.

Before noon she went down to the harbour with her father. While he
sought out Malan she made straight for *Blithe Spirit* with a list of last
minute tasks to run through. The place was frenetic with noise and
movement, dozens of men involved. Malan, rushed off his feet, spotted
her distant figure on the boat and commented 'That's not your co-
owner, surely?'

'He's a bit under the weather,' Mr Sellick agreed. 'We've got the next
generation instead. Knows all about boats and is a lot more agile.'

'As long as you're happy,' said Malan. 'Now then, that bloke over there
- he's the skipper of the tug that's pulling you across the Channel. I'll

make the introductions.'

The said skipper was a swarthy little chap named Bates, who'd done a lot of work in the London docks. He ground a fag out under his heel and pointed at a squat vessel 50 yards away. 'There she is, the little devil. She's called *Miranda*.'

'Oh brave new world that has such people in it,' intoned Mr Sellick, a lifelong fan of the bard.

'What?' said Bates.

'Sorry,' said Mr Sellick. 'What do I need to know?'

Bates observed him suspiciously. 'Have you been under tow before?'

'I haven't.'

'Hm. There's not much to it.' The skipper's expression said "If anyone could go wrong it would be a bungling little pipsqueak like you". 'I'll have four motor vessels under tow, including yours. Engine off, obviously – it's all about saving fuel. Keep an experienced man at the wheel. No sudden movements and try not to bang into people – especially not me.'

'What time are we likely to get under way?'

Bates looked at his watch. 'The way things are going, 10pm at the earliest. So it'll be pretty dark. No lights. We don't want to attract attention. If we really must have a light, I'll do it. Anything else?'

'Yes – how long will it take to get there?'

'Five hours minimum. We'll be doing route X. That'll mean bugger all to the likes of you, but ask your naval rating about it. Young Tyler – he'll know.'

Bates walked away. No handshake, or 'good luck', or even 'Damnation to all weekend sailors'.

In *Blithe Spirit* Chrissie was running through preparations for the journey. It was like the preliminaries for any of their trips, only more so. She saw that both anchors were secured, ropes coiled and fixed with light ties, the compass in its binnacle, navigation lights functioning. She checked the fenders, which on *Blithe Spirit* were a mixed bag of motorbike tyres. There were three life-jackets and three hard hats for the crew, all provided by the Admiralty.

When her father came on board he at once monitored the stuff she'd already checked. This was typical. On the boat he played the role of disciplinarian captain. Chrissie was used to it, which didn't stop her from getting cheesed off sometimes. Like now, when he finally hit on something she hadn't done.

'Is the bilge pump OK?'

'I've not checked yet.'

'Well get it done, Chrissie.'

'I know, I know.'

'Are you sure about that? You do realise this isn't our usual jaunt down the coast. This is serious. There'll be fighter planes, shells, all sorts. If we get hit, the pump will be crucial.'

She bit her lip. 'I'll do it now.'

'Make sure you do. What about the hatches?'

'I'll do them too.'

'Come on girl, pull yourself together.'

Later on they called home to get some food down. They'd intended to bid goodbye to Mrs Sellick but she wasn't about. It was unusual – she left the house less and less as her illness took hold – but not entirely a surprise. Chrissie's mother had a way of doing the awkward thing, especially if her own wishes had been flouted. What she *had* done was leave a large bag of food for them on the kitchen table. Another woman would have left a note with it. There was no time to go chasing after her and they returned to the boat.

The naval rating arrived after eight, as it was getting dark – a tall, remarkably composed young chap with a sheaf of charts and a droll expression. The first impression was a man of few words, the muttered introduction – 'Charles Tyler' – being one of his longer sentences. Chrissie had agreed to keep out of his way till the boats set off, so she waved a greeting from the cabin and Tyler went to help Bates with the towing lines. Then he returned to the wheel-house to take Mr Sellick through the charts.

The rating had drawn three separate routes on a chart depicting the Channel between England and France.

'The navigation's no big deal,' he said. 'There'll be so much traffic tonight we could almost follow other ships. But in case anything happens to me I'll talk you through it.'

'Why three different routes then?' asked Mr Sellick.

'I'll explain. A few days ago they started with this one – route 'Z'. It was quick – just 40 miles – but the ships copped so much shelling from batteries at Gravelines and Calais they had to give up. Then they tried route 'Y' – this one here – doubling back towards France at the Kwinte Buoy. That was better but it took too long.'

'So we're doing route 'X'?', said Mr Sellick.

'Right. Today's May 31st, isn't it. We're a bit late joining the action, but it does mean we can benefit from the earlier experiences. We make for the North Goodwin lighthouse, then go south-east, then due south at the Ruytingen Pass. Fifty-five miles all told. The minesweepers have cleared the way. Still some shelling from Gravelines but it's a lot easier.'

Soon after that they got under way. Mr Sellick took the wheel as Bates shouted instructions through a loud-hailer on the tug. There were four vessels under tow, two lines of two with *Blithe Spirit* at the back on the right. Once they'd negotiated the harbour exit there was little for towed vessels to do, except avoid their immediate neighbours. The convoy forged on in darkness at a steady 10 knots. And now Mr Sellick could relax about having Chrissie on board. Her eventual discovery was inevitable, but there was no way the convoy would turn back once under way.

As it happened Chrissie's identity emerged quickly. As soon as they were out of the harbour she left the cabin to join the other two in the wheel-house. The girl's fair features were camouflaged by darkness, but something about her stature and way of moving attracted Tyler's attention.

'So this is your son?' he said.

Mr Sellick couldn't deny the deception but was averse to outright lying. 'I'm the father all right,' he replied, with studied ambiguity.

'Hmm.' Tyler subjected Chrissie to a second inspection. 'It's funny how a father's physique doesn't always pass down to the son.'

'Appearances can be deceptive,' said Mr Sellick. 'Chris is a tough little bugger.'

'All right then.' Tyler was suddenly animated. 'Arm wrestling. We do a lot that with newcomers in the R.N.'

'I don't want any horse-play on board,' said Mr Sellick.

But Tyler was already rolling up his sleeve. On *Blithe Spirit* the matter of authority lacked the customary rigidity of ships at sea. Mr Sellick owned the boat, but Tyler was the navy employee, the Admiralty's man. Add to that the special circumstances of Operation Dynamo, with its fly-by-night quality. Chrissie settled things by rolling up her own sleeve.

'Fine by me,' she growled, in an approximation of a male voice.

They knelt on the wheel-house floor with elbows planted on the raised deck by the entrance. The struggle was fierce but brief. Chrissie could have taken on most women and even an out-of-shape man, but not a naval rating.

'All right, you win,' she admitted, in her normal tone of voice.

Tyler did a double-take. 'Good god, a girl!'

'Kind of you to notice.'

'In which case that wasn't at all bad,' said Tyler.

They scrambled to their feet. 'You don't mind, then?' said Chrissie.

'Mind what?'

'Having a *female* as a shipmate.'

'It's unusual, but all that matters is competence. I've worked with some chaps who couldn't leave harbour without hitting a wall.' He rolled his sleeve down. 'It'll happen one day.'

'What will?'

'Men and women side by side on Royal Navy ships.'

'You think so?'

'Of course. Not for decades though. We're still in the dark ages.'

Chrissie shook her head, unnoticed in the gloom. 'I know what you mean.'

Mr Sellick heard the exchange with mixed feelings. He felt relieved that Chrissie's identity wasn't going to cause problems. Yet if his two crew members hit it off he'd be marginalised, older than them and out of things. It couldn't be helped. He was back in his boat, on the ocean, and that was what mattered.

'Is it OK if I make us some tea?' Tyler asked him.

'It's very OK,' said Mr Sellick. 'The stuff's down in the galley.'

Tyler vanished into the cabin and returned with three mugs of tea on a tray, negotiating the steps up to the wheel-house like the regular he was. Another point in the rating's favour, Chrissie thought – that he hadn't assumed *the female* would make tea. Mr Sellick stayed at the wheel while she and Tyler drank outside, leaning against the guard-rail. They spoke little, which Chrissie also appreciated. Being in the boat engendered her usual sense of peace and belonging. That the circumstances were so singular only added to her happiness. She liked the sound of the sea slapping *Blithe Spirit's* hull and the queer throbbing of the tug's engines ahead. She liked the black night and the inchoate forms of other boats and the suggestion of a line where the sea met a clouded sky. The uncertainty, the prospect of danger, stirred an excitement unlike anything she'd experienced.

Tyler spoke beside her. 'This sea – it's uncanny.'

'It's calm.'

'Yes, more than I've ever seen. No wind. You know what a bastard the Channel can be.'

'Like it's been held back just for us – for what we have to do.'

'I was thinking that. And clouds are good.'

'Are they?' she said.

'They keep the fighters away.'

'Of course. I should have thought of that.'

'Do you feel scared?'

'I know I should, but no. I feel great.'

'I thought so. You don't look scared.' Tyler peered into the distance and moved sharply towards the sliding door of the wheel-house. 'Better get inside.'

'What's up?'

'You'll see. Quick.'

Within seconds she saw very clearly. A destroyer was surging back from Dunkirk on its way to Dover, doing more than 20 knots, she surmised. Whether Bates had relaxed his 'no lights' rule to advertise the convoy's presence wasn't clear, because the ship passed quite close enough to them. As the great dark form went past she felt its power and glimpsed the deck crammed with troops. But then came the after-shock: the fierce wash that had *Blithe Spirit* bucking crazily on the surface and seawater spattering the windows of the wheel-house. She remembered Uncle Stephen warning about this danger, and easily visualised a small boat overturning in such circumstances.

Mr Sellick stayed at the wheel and the other two returned outside to lean against the guard rail, with the deck now streaming wet under their feet. The talk remained intermittent yet Chrissie was surprised how easily it flowed. It was not her usual experience with men, apart from the saloon-bar banter of the Vale Road Tavern. Not that Tyler was a man she'd ever fancy, and besides she heard all about the girl-friend in Northampton, to whom he was obviously devoted. No, his appeal was more subtle, his attitude more free thinking than the blokes she'd known. He had an intellectual curiosity that was reminiscent of her father's. And against expectation his future ambitions did not include the Navy; he had a yen to tread the boards as a song-and-dance man, an aspiration she found oddly touching. Not for the first time it occurred to Chrissie that the 21 years of her life had been pretty sheltered, passed in a town with its own agreeable little ways but far from the cosmopolitan milieu of a big city. And now...along came one junior naval rating and her horizons were instantly challenged.

Though she relished being back on *Blithe Spirit*, the journey to France did involve a distinct element of monotony: the same sombre sights, the same sounds, the same feel of the sea under her feet hour after hour, redeemed by sightings of ships returning laden from Dunkirk. She and her father and Tyler took undemanding turns at the wheel, talked a little, drank more tea. But towards the end of the fourth hour one episode changed all that.

Fortunately all three of them were in the wheel-house at the time. One moment the boat was moving forward in darkness. In the next there was a tremendous explosion ahead and a sheet of fire pierced the night, illuminating a thousand details on the surface of the sea. Mr Sellick dropped a mug which smashed on the wheel-house floor. Chrissie caught a momentary snapshot of a man in the boat nearest to them as he turned open-mouthed towards the conflagration. The column of flame plunged sizzling into the deep. After that came quietness, as the tug's engines were silenced; and the steady forward motion of the previous four hours stopped along with them.

There were shouts from men in the other three boats under tow, but Mr Sellick's voice rang out above them. 'Start the engines, Chrissie. I'll do the lamps. Get the torches.'

She obeyed as though in a dream world, and to her relief heard the familiar sound of *Blithe Spirit's* engines responding. Mr Sellick lit two paraffin lamps, which did little to illuminate the scene. He and Tyler were already on deck, leaning over the rail to shine torches into the depths.

'Hold her steady, Chrissie,' came her father's voice. 'We want to be where the tug was at the moment of explosion.'

Mr Sellick had been the first to realise what happened and the first to react. Now the silence was broken by the sound of part-time skippers trying to start their engines, with varying success. The small boats activated every light they had, regardless of potential danger from the air. They clustered together with the men peering into the inky water, unable to credit that a tug could vanish in a few seconds. The parted tow ropes that led individually to each boat were the only clue *Miranda* had been there at all. Not one piece of debris remained on the surface to validate her existence.

'Are you all right, Chrissie?' came Mr Sellick's voice.

'I am, dad.' Her voice was shaky. 'I just...I can't believe what's happened.'

'I know. Tyler – you OK?'

'OK skipper.'

'That had to be a mine,' said Mr Sellick. 'What a bastard.'

'Magnetic,' Tyler suggested.

'Poor Bates,' said Mr Sellick. 'Can't say he was my favourite person – he was a pain in the butt. He didn't deserve that though. Hope he had a fag in his mouth when it went down – that's how he'd have liked to go.'

They hung about for ten minutes shouting to men in the other boats. One had failed to start her engine, and the skipper said they'd stick around waiting for a tow back to Britain. The other two wondered aloud whether they could navigate their way to Dunkirk.

'We'll have a go, shall we?' Mr Sellick said, calling to the other boats to follow, whereupon they fell in line behind *Blithe Spirit* and cut their lights. Mr Sellick and Tyler stayed at the wheel, constantly glancing at the compass.

It was still dark and they were at least an hour from Dunkirk, but Chrissie had absolute faith in her father's ability to get there. She'd seen him in action many times before. Tyler too seemed to know what he was doing. Even so, finding the entrance to the harbour proved a tricky affair. They were aided by a glimmer of dawn light, then by the unparalleled silhouette of the port itself, with flames rising from its burning oil tanks and blazing buildings in the town beyond. The fierce residue of burning oil invaded their nostrils and tormented their eyes.

'By god,' said Mr Sellick. 'It's a kind of hell in there.'

'Let's give thanks for the burning oil though,' Tyler said. 'Keeps the Luftwaffe away. That and the low cloud.'

As it happened they didn't have to enter the harbour. An officer stood on the end of the breakwater with loud-hailer in hand and bellowed down to them.

'Ahoy there, *Blithe Spirit*. Welcome to Dunkirk.'

'To Hades, more like,' muttered Mr Sellick.

'Just you and one other?' came the hailer.

Mr Sellick turned and peered into the murk behind. 'Good god, we've lost another one.'

'Five set out and two arrive,' Chrissie said mournfully.

'Don't come into the harbour,' cried the hailer. 'They need you blokes on the beaches. Find a big ship lying off the coast – destroyer, mine-sweeper, whatever. Pick up men from the beaches and deliver them. Keep at it for as long as you've got fuel to spare. You know about the geography here?'

'Tell us,' said Mr Sellick.

'There's a deep water channel 800 yards wide, running from the shallows. Goes many miles along the coast. Keep to that because beyond it you'll find serious sandbanks.'

'Got it,' said Mr Sellick.

'Good luck and thanks for coming.'

The instructions, simple enough, were far from simple to carry out.

They found their destroyer, the *Ivanhoe*, then moved towards the beach. The chart showed four small towns – in normal times, seaside resorts – along an eight-mile stretch: Malo-les-Bains, Zuydcoote, Bray-Dunes and La Panne. Beyond La Panne were the Germans. They cruised towards land, and none of them would forget their first sight of what was going on there.

'Bloody hell,' said Tyler, the first dubious word they'd heard from his young lips.

'I don't believe it,' said Chrissie.

From a distance, the stretch of sand they could see was covered with black lines running parallel to each other, from the dunes to the sea. It looked as if low tide was an hour or two behind them, but even so the gradual shelving of the beach – across a big distance – was self-evident. As *Blithe Spirit* progressed, the black lines turned themselves into columns of men, in numbers that were unfathomable – and even then they represented merely the men within sight. Moving nearer still they saw that the leading figures of each column were in the water, mostly up to their waists or even their shoulders.

'Take the wheel, Chrissie,' said Mr Sellick, 'And be very careful. We mustn't get beached here. You can see how far to go in by where the sea comes on the men's bodies. Keep the bows facing the sands. Tyler – you and I stand one each side helping them on board. One man at a time. At all costs avoid lots of the buggers climbing the same side together, 'cos that's a sure way to get us overturned.'

As with most of the weekend sailors this was a process they'd not had to handle before, but all things considered their first effort went tolerably well. Mr Sellick shouted instructions and most of the troops did what he said. What the *Blithe Spirit* crew hadn't reckoned on was the poor physical condition of these men, who'd walked for miles with little in the way of food and water. They were weighed down by waterlogged clothes and heavy boots, and being soldiers, were unfamiliar with boats and their ticklish ways. Tyler was magnificent with them, manifesting an uncomplicated strength as he hauled man after man aboard. Chrissie worried about her father, but he too showed both strength and an unexpected cunning in the way he handled the boarders. Even so there were times when she wanted to ignore her orders and give him a helping hand, but without putting down the anchor she couldn't leave the wheel. The harrowed expressions of the men in the sea kept all three of them up to the mark.

Chrissie was the one who directed troops to different parts of the boat, starting with the cabin, then the deck above it. To her surprise most men still carried rifles, and a growing pile mounted on the wheel-house floor. Finally she backed *Blithe Spirit* away from the shore – though troops still in the sea begged her not to – turned her round and made for the *Ivanhoe* to offload. She reckoned they'd taken on board at least 25 men.

Her father and Tyler joined her at the wheel. Nothing was said but she knew from their expressions that both were pleased. She felt it too. They'd combined as a team and brought off a difficult undertaking – though it wasn't finished until the troops were safely on another ship.

'May I suggest something, skip?' said Tyler, the soul of tact.

'Of course.'

'Those men are dehydrated. They say there's no decent water supply in Dunkirk.'

'Of course,' said Mr Sellick again, nodding towards his daughter. She filled a bucket from one of the water tanks and took it to the cabin. The sight of the place depressed her: a dozen or more men lolling silent and grim-faced on the floor with no spark of life. It brought home to her what they'd had to endure.

Nonetheless the sight of her rear end descending the steps reminded the Tommies of their reputation for irreverent banter.

'Miss, miss, over here miss.'

'Don't give it to him miss – he's a sergeant.'

'I've enough water for everyone,' she called out, 'So please be patient.' She went from one man to the next, allowing each to drink from a pitcher, which they took like men possessed. One by one the soldiers rallied and called out wisecracks, nothing much more than she'd heard in the saloon bar of the Ramsgate Tavern.

'It'll go down better if you sit on my knee, miss.'

'Will you marry me, miss. I'm coming into some money when I'm 21.'

'Ave you got any warm beer, miss?'

'Is that really a woman or 'ave I gone to heaven?'

Exhausted and wet and often injured, the men looked terrible. Even so the presence of an upbeat young woman gave them a lift. Chrissie knew it and relished the feeling. She might well have gone in for nursing had she not been so capable with machines.

After she'd provided for the men up on deck, she returned to Tyler and her father. The *Ivanhoe* was visible in the distance and they moved steadily towards it. 'These poor blokes are dog-tired,' she said. 'They'll be glad of a comfortable berth on a bigger ship.'

'Actually they'd prefer to go to Blighty on this one,' said Tyler.

'Why do you say that?'

'Destroyers aren't designed to carry men,' Tyler explained. 'I know because I've worked on them. There's little spare space below deck. You've got a small wardroom and the officers' cabins – men could go in there I suppose. Amidships, the engines. Boilers for'ard. The mess decks are pretty small for the existing crew, believe me. Men like these will mostly be put up on deck. Makes the ships very unstable. They'll list terribly.'

'Their funeral,' said Mr Sellick.

When they reached the *Ivanhoe* the soldiers' poor condition showed up again. The destroyer had nets and rope ladders down its side but soldiers were unused to such things and progress to the deck was slow. One man got stuck, dangling like a fly in a spider's web, to be hauled up on a rope by a sailor. It was some while before *Blithe Spirit* had transferred its load. Eventually they were ready.

'Back to the beach then,' said Mr Sellick.

Chrissie and Tyler exchanged glances. They'd done one trip in 90 minutes and taken just 25 men off the sands.

As their boat drew away from the destroyer's side another moved in to take its place. Chrissie gave it a glance, then a double-take. It was like no other vessel she'd seen since leaving Ramsgate: a long, low, flat affair with a bright red, raised cabin extending half its 80-foot length. Dozens of troops stood shoulder to shoulder on deck, and similar numbers must have been inside. A crew of at least ten men were in an unfamiliar uniform.

'What on earth is that?' she said.

Tyler chuckled. 'It's the *Massey Shaw*.'

'I know that, clever clogs – I can read too. But *what* is it?'

'A fire boat. Belongs to the London Fire Brigade. Normally operates on the Thames – can't imagine what she's doing out here. Though come to think of it she'll be useful on the beaches. For her size the *Massey Shaw's* got a pretty shallow draft.'

Chrissie stared at him. 'How do you know all this?'

Tyler looked a bit embarrassed. 'I'm interested in stuff like that.'

'But you're a song-and-dance man!'

'Think of it as my hobby.'

Chrissie shook her head. 'Sad.'

Stranger sights met their eyes as *Blithe Spirit* approached the sands for a second time. Some soldiers had tired of waiting for boats and devised Heath-Robinson alternatives of their own. They passed two men sitting in inflated inner tubes taken from some large vehicle, using their rifles to paddle. They were doing better than another pair, who paddled a collapsible boat half-full of sea-water.

'Help us, we're sinking,' called one of the men, not altogether seriously.

They were ignored, except that Mr Sellick shouted 'Use your helmets to bail'.

At the beach this time round, Chrissie's attention went beyond the desperate men in the water to the broader picture, and it didn't inspire confidence. All kinds of abandoned motor transports littered the sands. At the water's edge were various rowing boats, grounded or capsized, with a defunct motor boat in their midst, a grim warning about their own endeavours. Several wrecks were submerged in the surrounding waters.

Mr Sellick pointed to another feature. A freshening onshore wind had blown up, swelling the waves to little white crests, a change from the miraculously calm sea that had favoured their journey from England. It wouldn't normally have been a problem, but now caused serious difficulties for small boats trying to lift men from the shallows. The dangers were exemplified as a gruesome tragedy played out before their eyes. A hundred yards ahead a whaler was drawn by a motorboat towards a gaggle of troops in the sea. Instead of an orderly boarding routine there was a rush of men towards the small vessel, with half-a-dozen trying to haul themselves over the gunwales at the same time. Chrissie heard the panicky shouts of two sailors in the whaler and saw the boat turn turtle, depositing the lot of them in the drink. The sailor's heads soon broke the surface as they clung to the upturned hull, but most of the soldiers went down and failed to reappear. With a shock she realised that exhausted men were drowning in a few feet of water, as quietly and terminally as the crew of the *Miranda* had gone to their watery grave.

'I don't like the look of this,' said Mr Sellick, surveying soldiers still up to their chests in the sea, clamouring for attention.

Tyler stiffened. 'Those uniforms. That's not the British army, surely.'

'Oh no!' said Mr Sellick. 'Those are the French buggers.'

'I see.' For the first time since Ramsgate, Tyler looked uncertain. 'So do we take them. sir? I mean, it's not the same, is it?'

'Come on, dad,' Chrissie urged. 'They're people. They're on our side.'

'So they tell me.' Still Mr Sellick hesitated. 'All right then,' he said eventually. 'But don't stand any nonsense.'

They approached the task in the same way as before, but it soon became clear that French troops were less malleable than the British. They ignored Mr Sellick's shouted instructions and a dozen of them fanned out along one side of *Blithe Spirit* and began clawing at the hull.

'No, no, no!' cried Mr Sellick. '*Attendrez-vous. La-bas! La-bas!*'

The men ignored him, as others had ignored sailors in the whaler a few moments before. Within seconds seven or eight of them were clinging to the hull attempting to haul themselves on board, and *Blithe Spirit* rocked perilously. The sudden danger took Chrissie's breath away. She was about to take the boat aft to try and shake men off, when she noticed her father delve into his clothing and approach the officer of the group. Mr Sellick shouted in French, a language which – to Chrissie's knowledge – he didn't speak.

'*Arretez-vous, ou je tirer.*'

She saw the pistol pointing at the officer's head, yet the man still scrabbled at the hull. When it came, the loud report made her jump clean off the deck. More to the point the officer relinquished his grasp, and so did most of the men with him.

'Now do as you're told you fucking Froggy half-wit,' Mr Sellick bellowed in a fearsome voice. 'The next shot will go through your fucking head.'

His passion, completely out of character, secured an immediate reaction, and the Frenchmen stayed back awaiting instructions. Mr Sellick shrugged towards his daughter. 'Useful to have a few words of the language.'

After that the French followed orders, more or less, and as far as language differences would allow. The boat got its load, though dragging those men on board was fraught with difficulty. Most of them wore greatcoats and many had packs on their backs, plus in several cases rolled-up blankets. Conspicuously absent were their rifles. Mr Sellick took on fewer boarders than the previous time and treated those he had with restraint. The mood was chilly as *Blithe Spirit* beat a path back to the *Ivanhoe*. The crew remained tight-lipped, except that Tyler turned to his skipper in open admiration and said 'That was fantastic, sir.'

Chrissie's thoughts were all over the place. Who was this man who'd been around all her life and so often dominated her thoughts? He'd used several French terms, though she was almost sure he spoke no languages; dammit, he hated the French – had often said he'd sign up to fight against them. And he'd said another word, more surprising than any French expression, one she'd never heard from his lips in 21 years, and that she herself wouldn't dare use at home. As if these things were not enough her father had also conjured a gun from somewhere, like a magician pulling a rabbit from a hat.

She turned to him at the wheel. 'Dad, the pistol...where...how?'

'I know,' was all he would say. 'Don't tell your mother.'

Chrissie moved away, wishing – as so often before – that her feelings for him were better reciprocated.

As their dodgy French cargo was delivered to the *Ivanhoe*, they had a bit of luck. The crew felt badly in need of a breathing space before returning to the beaches, and the destroyer's captain came on deck to provide one. He told them the use of unpowered boats at Dunkirk had been carelessly handled; that too often these craft had been allowed to drift away after offloading troops from the beaches, instead of being retained for further use. So *Blithe Spirit* moved off with a new mandate, and after an hour they returned to deliver a couple of whalers and a skiff, all found drifting off the coast.

A second piece of luck came courtesy of the *Ivanhoe* captain, who seemed a very practical sort of bloke. He told them there were points along the sands where 'piers' had been thrown together so troops could board boats more easily on the shelving beaches. What was more he described exactly where to find one. Mr Sellick immediately set a course for it.

Midway between Malo-les-Bains and Zuydcoote they found the pier, formed from a string of half-a-dozen lorries. These had been driven into the sea at low tide by Sappers, to form a platform when the waters flooded back. A variety of planks and other materials had been secured along the top. Lines of English and French troops queued on the sands in a fairly orderly fashion, and a couple of small boats stood by to receive them.

When *Blithe Spirit's* turn came, the transfer of troops was a piece of cake compared to what had gone before. They made a light mooring to the last lorry and men simply walked the length of the pier and dropped down into the boat. The most incompetent landlubber could have managed it. There was a tricky confrontation when the boat filled up, and Mr Sellick cut off the flow of men. He and Tyler had to raise their voices but the pistol didn't come out.

They were about to cast off when a young sailor made a surprise appearance at the end of the pier. Despite his youth – early 20s at most – he carried an air of authority.

'Need any help, sir?'

'I think we're OK, thanks,' said Mr Sellick. 'Who are you?'

'Vic Viner.' The sailor squeezed onto the boat and shook hands. 'Leading Seaman Viner, if you need the full title.'

Mr Sellick introduced Chrissie and Tyler. 'Surprised to find a sailor on shore,' he said. 'What's your role here?'

'Good question,' said Viner. 'I came out on the *Esk* – destroyer – and they put me on the beach. Must've upset someone in authority. There are nearly a hundred of us along these sands. We're called "beachmasters". The idea is to give out information to the troops and try and keep order.'

'That's a job and a half!' said Mr Sellick. 'How long have you been here?'

'Five days, sir. And five nights, of course.'

'Good lord. Well, I can confirm there's a need for information all right. No doubt about it.'

'Yes sir. Nobody knows what's going on.' Viner turned to wave back two soldiers who looked as if they were about to jump on board. 'Full up here, mate. You need to get back in line.'

'Exactly,' said Mr Sellick. 'That can be a problem.' He described the trouble they'd had with French soldiers in the shallows. 'You said about keeping order. Can you actually do that?'

Viner patted his pocket. 'They've issued me with a revolver for when men try to jump the queue, and things of that sort. I've drawn it three times so far. Haven't had to fire. I would, though.'

'I know what you mean,' said Mr Sellick grimly.

'The French are a pain, sir. Too much gear, and they won't leave anything behind. Language problems, of course. And back there in the harbour...' – he pointed over his shoulder towards billows of black smoke in the sky – 'They tell me the Froggies won't be split up from their units. Insist they all get on the same ship together. It's a nightmare. Can't blame them in a way. It's their country and they're demoralised. We've got to take them, like it or not. It seems Churchill has ordered our ships to take one Froggy for every Englishman.'

'We'll see about that,' said Mr Sellick. 'Look, you're doing an important job here and I wish you every good fortune. You must feel very exposed when the Luftwaffe move in.'

Viner put a finger to his lips. 'Shush, please sir. We've had a bit of machine gun fire and some dive-bombing, but not so much. I reckon the Krauts are missing a trick there. Long may it last.'

Chrissie had gone back into the boat, and now stepped forward proffering a pitcher of water. Viner took it without a word and drank deeply. He handed back the pitcher, gazing steadfastly at Chrissie, who didn't seem to mind.

'Didn't expect to see a woman out here. Angel of mercy.'

Something made Mr Sellick enquire 'You're not married, I suppose.'

'Funny you should ask that, sir – I was spliced three weeks ago back in Blighty. Winnie – a lovely girl. Wouldn't mind setting eyes on her now.'

'I bet you wouldn't.' Mr Sellick looked at him. 'War....what a bugger, eh?'

'Yes sir.'

Soldiers on the pier were getting restive and Mr Sellick knew it was time to leave. They wished Leading Seaman Viner 'Good luck' and Tyler cast off the line. At the last minute Viner remembered something.

'Don't go down the beaches as far as La Panne, sir. It's in German hands now. They're setting up machine guns in the dunes.'

Blithe Spirit was less than a hundred yards away when they heard the roar of aeroplane engines, and troops on the beach scattered towards the dunes. Even at a distance they could see the sand kicking up.

'He spoke a bit too soon,' observed Mr Sellick. 'Impressive young chap, that. Hopes he makes it.'

Finding the pier was a plus, and helped them to speed up the transfer of troops. The routine they'd fallen into was sustained almost without thinking. Had someone asked Chrissie how many times they'd shuttled back and forth she'd have been unable to say. They were ridiculously weary, but the pressing need for small boats kept them at it as long as there was fuel to spare. They snatched a snack and a drink of tea as the boat returned to the beaches, but that was the limit of any personal refuelling.

There was no let-up in the distant sound of artillery coming from the harbour, but the channel of sea where the big ships lay offshore had been less affected by the German onslaught. Occasionally they saw attacks by bombers and/or fighters, but managed to stay out of trouble themselves. That all changed just before 8am, when Mr Sellick had started thinking about the return journey. They'd just delivered a batch of English and French troops to a minesweeper off Bray-Dunes when the destroyer *Keith* came charging down the channel, weaving all over the place, pursued by several dive bombers. Mr Sellick took *Blithe Spirit* clear of any conceivable collision, but couldn't resist hanging around to see what transpired. The destroyer didn't appear to be directly hit but a bomb had gone off astern, after which she started going round in circles.

'What's she up to now?' cried Chrissie, excited despite herself.

'That last explosion must have jammed her steering,' Tyler explained. 'It's all she can do now to evade the bombs.'

'But she's not firing back – I don't think so.'

'No, that is odd. My guess is she's been out here so long her ammo's used up. She's a sitting duck.'

They watched as more bombers dived and the *Keith* was hit several times to starboard. Flames sprang out of the steam and smoke that billowed from the stricken vessel. Chrissie saw a man trapped in the flames whose clothes exploded as ammunition in his pockets caught fire.

'The engine room's on fire,' said Tyler. 'This is awful. Not long now.'

Mr Sellick was fidgeting. 'I'm sorry you two, but we ought to move away from this.'

'Just a few minutes, dad,' urged Chrissie. 'After all, maybe we'll be able to help survivors.'

He grinned. 'Don't be daft, girl. There's a couple of tugs moving in now – look.' They saw the *Vincia* and *St.Abbs* go in close to pick up the *Keith's* crew. 'All right then,' Mr Sellick relented, 'A few minutes more.' He was as fascinated as the other two.

'They've abandoned ship,' cried Tyler.

The *Keith* was listing heavily to port, with her upper deck almost under water. Chrissie took the binoculars and could see men thrashing about in the oily sea. More bombs fell amongst them as a new wave of planes dived in, for good measure machine-gunning the survivors. Meanwhile the mine-sweeper *Skipjack*, which had also gone to help, was struck by bombs. She turned over and briefly floated upside down before sinking. Someone had stayed at the *Skipjack's* guns until the last moments, because a Stuka plunged into the sea a hundred yards away. This made Chrissie look at the sky, which was marked far and wide by the blotches of bursting shells and teeming with aircraft of all descriptions As she watched, a fighter collided with a bomber and both crews baled out.

Tracers ripped into one of the parachutes as it came down. The tail section of a plane tumbled down to join wreckage littering the ocean's surface. Everywhere were pools of oil marking the demise of ships. And now the *St.Abbs*, which had picked up survivors from the *Keith*, was hit by a single bomb as she manoeuvred this way and that; she disintegrated within a minute, leaving dozens more men struggling in the waves.

Chrissie watched it all with conflicting emotions. She was an unsentimental person, rarely known to cry, yet she felt the devastation being dealt out and the pain and misery that went with it; the *Skipjack* would have gone down with hundreds of men trapped within its hull. For that matter she knew everyone on *Blithe Spirit* could be wiped out by a single bomb. Still she couldn't help responding to the panorama of destruction. Her weariness fell away. Her body tingled. She felt exhilarated by it – and couldn't help herself. Glancing across the boat, Chrissie saw her father's expression and wondered if he'd guessed her thoughts. To distract him, she spoke up.

'Sorry, dad – you're right. We do need to get away.'

Mr Sellick smiled inscrutably and set a course for the beach. 'OK then. One last time, one last pick-up – then we head for home. We're getting a bit low on fuel and besides...' He scanned the skies. 'I don't like the way those clouds have shifted. The last thing we want is a clear sky to encourage Boche fighters.'

'Amen to that,' murmured Tyler.

He took *Blithe Spirit* to their usual pier. A gaggle of British soldiers were on the sands. No sign of the French.

'We don't want too many,' he told Chrissie and Tyler. 'This lot'll be coming all the way to Ramsgate with us. Let's hope we get some decent types.'

An untidy cheer came from the troops as the boat berthed. They took fifteen men inside the cabin and another ten on the deck above, and made it clear that people must stay where they were put; actually the troops had been waiting 24 hours and would have agreed to anything. They cast off leaving plenty of men still on the beach, and ran parallel to the coast. The smudge of burning harbour dominated the distant view. Mr Sellick was about to move out to sea when Chrissie gave a shout.

'Look – let's get those two!'

A beached motor-boat lay at the edge of the sands in three feet of water. Her name, *Malden Annie IV*, was clearly visible on the hull. On her deck stood two men, both the worse for wear, the smaller one leaning heavily against his companion. Nobody else was near.

'We have a full complement, Chrissie,' said Mr Sellick.

'One of those blokes is injured. He can't stand properly.'

'There'll be other boats. We're full up.'

The taller man waved – not frantically, as many troops did – but with a measured calmness.

'Could we get them sir?' said Tyler. 'We can be be in and out in a few minutes.'

Mr Sellick sighed, looking from one member of his crew to the other. 'I promise you one thing. If we get beached on this stretch of sand, you two will be the ones to get out and push.'

~ Five ~

Arthur started the motor and took the bike through the centre of the village, with Joseph in his customary place behind. Looking back on the accident afterwards – which he did hundreds of times – he wished he'd taken things more slowly, though in truth their speed wasn't excessive. By the time he'd noticed the oil patch it was too late. There were a few seconds of a helpless, out-of-control sensation before he surrendered to his fate. The BSA skidded 20 yards and fetched up against the base of an iron lamp-post. He knew immediately from the pain that his luck had run out.

Joseph was the more fortunate of the two, because their unexpected trajectory threw him backwards off the bike. He lost consciousness for a few seconds and came to at the roadside, unsure where he was or what had happened. The sound of an engine made him look up from the tarmac. A few yards away Arthur lay half-pinioned by the bike, which had its engine still running. Joseph stood and moved shakily towards him, but wasn't the first to get there.

What Arthur registered, after the pain in his leg, was a soothing warmth against his face, as if someone was applying a moist flannel. He opened his eyes and saw Lag, tail wagging, mouth open, pink tongue lolling. He heard Joseph's voice and felt the bike being pulled off his legs.

'Are *you* OK?' Arthur asked, and Joseph was never to forget that, especially when the full circumstances were clear.

'I think so, but not so sure about you.'

'What about the bike?' The first concern of any Don R.

'You don't want to know,' said Joseph, contemplating the front wheel, bent to an extraordinary shape.

The stream of abuse that followed would have shaken a dock-worker, let alone a Methodist. But now Joseph noticed the state of his friend's foot.

'Let me see that. Out of the way, Lag.'

'It's no use, Jos.'

Arthur's lower right leg had been crushed between the bike and the road surface. His boot and sock had come off, revealing a swollen, bloody foot beneath.

'So we're going back to the house,' said Joseph

He helped Arthur to sit up, then dragged him upright. The injured man put his foot to the ground and gave a yell of pain. He returned to the house by hopping, leaning against Joseph's shoulder. After a few yards they stopped and Joseph stooped to hand the torn-off boot to Lag. The dog scampered self-importantly alongside, boot in mouth.

After what had happened, the familiar contours of the house were a welcome sight. Joseph settled his friend in an armchair and put on the kettle. When Arthur had a cuppa in hand he washed the blood from the injured leg and took a closer look. Where the contusions were worst the skin had an unhealthy bluish look, and a glimpse of bone was visible underneath.

'How much does it hurt?' Joseph asked.

'It hurts, but I can put up with that. Trouble is I can't walk on it.'

Joseph knew nothing whatsoever about first aid and said so.

'Forget it, mate,' said Arthur. 'I'm buggered. Something's broken – I can feel it. You'll have to go on alone now.'

'On my own! Oh, you think so?'

'Course. No point both of us getting stuck in this godforsaken hole.' He settled back expansively in the armchair. 'I quite fancy a spot of rest, actually. I've got the ham. I've got Lag for company.' He patted the dog's head.

Joseph perched on the arm of the chair and stared down at its occupant. 'Arthur, let's get this straight. Where I go, you go. I am *not* leaving you behind. You don't seriously think I'd do that?'

'Bloody right mate, I'd leave *you*, no problem. You *must* go. In fact – I don't want to pull rank, but I order you to go.' He pointed to the corporal's stripes on his arm. 'So don't get uppity with me.'

Joseph's roar of laughter was completely unforced. 'Pipe down you daft 'ha'p'orth, and start thinking how we're going to do this. You're supposed to be a resourceful sort of character.'

'I can't walk, I tell you. And the bike's kaput. You can't *carry* me to the coast.'

'Can't, can't, can't.' Joseph pointed a finger. 'Stay there.'

He went into the garden and returned two minutes later wheeling the woman's bike, previously seen in the shed nestling against a lawnmower. He pointed to it with a little flourish.

'So. When do you want to start? Tomorrow?'

'Now,' said Arthur, executing a complete volte face without explanation.

'Really? You don't need some time to recover?'

'If we're going – let's do it now.'

'OK, come on then.'

The bicycle had a pump clipped to its frame, so they began with the tyres full of air. While not exactly straightforward, progress was easier than either man had imagined. It bore some resemblance to a three-legged race, a favourite amongst children's games. Joseph pushed at the handlebars, while Arthur rested the injured leg on one pedal and pushed at the ground with the other.

'It's not so bad,' said Joseph.

'Wait till we go up-hill,' said Arthur.

'Wait till you go *down*-hill,' said Joseph.

After a hundred yards they were overtaken by a familiar form. Lag had left the back garden by the usual route, whatever that was, and came alongside wearing an 'I belong with you' expression.

'He'd be safer staying at the house,' said Arthur.

'He's made his decision,' said Joseph. 'He's thrown his lot in with us.'

'So be it then.'

Arthur reckoned they had 20 miles to cover before Dunkirk. He was thinking clearly despite pain from the leg. At every intersection he knew spontaneously which way to go – a Don R's instinct. After an hour Joseph spotted – miraculous to relate – a French first-aid post, civilian variety, operating from a village hall. He wondered if they'd be willing to treat two English soldiers but the man let them in, saying he knew '*un peu d'Anglais*'. Faced with Arthur's leg he muttered and shook his head and made the 'pr-pr-pr-pr' sound, but then fitted a rudimentary splint on it. Best of all he handed over what they assumed were a dozen pain-killers. Joseph's opinion of the French nation took a sharp turn to the good. He was beginning to appreciate that survival in war depended upon small pieces of luck, random decisions, a sympathetic face here and there. And having Lag along helped, because the French doctor made a fuss of him.

If they were tempted to dwell on their own misfortune the tragedy of the French nation shook them out of it. In mid-afternoon they saw a man burying his child in the back garden; heard the bleak sound of spade striking rock and registered the expression on the father's face.

Their second bit of luck was finding a functioning bakery in the next village. Arthur went into his bartering routine, securing a fresh loaf for some notes of local currency plus some ham from the saddle-bag. They waited for the loaf to come out warm from the oven while the baker gave them water and some scraps for Lag. It would have been criminal to let the bread get cold, so they made for a cemetery beside the village church. Arthur sat with his back against a gravestone and his leg up (as the medic had advised) on a nearby sepulchre.

They disposed of the loaf plus more of the ham, while Lag made movements suggesting he should participate. It was a peaceful scene removed from any indication that war was all around. The mouldering gravestones, half-buried in creepers and tangled undergrowth, mostly dated from the World War 1 era.

Some sheets of paper were scattered about the cemetery and Joseph picked one up.

'You're surrounded, give up,' he read aloud, adding more text that outlined the disposition of German forces in the area. 'Hm, good English, these Germans.'

'Typical,' grumbled Arthur. 'Better than anything our brass could come up with.'

They took to the road again. Lag was their advance party, prospecting the route, stopping to look back, waiting till they caught up with him again. The few people they met were French refugees, friendly but utterly dejected. No British soldiers made an appearance for an hour or more, due to Arthur's instinct for keeping to the country lanes. It couldn't last, and there came the moment when the route they were on fed into a major trunk road. At once the landscape was full of British troops, all heading in the same direction – a remarkable transformation. Joseph was struck by the variations in their approach to the journey. Some units had stuck together and marched in formation under an officer, rifles on shoulders, striking the sort of pace he remembered from square-bashing days – but they were the exception. Most men were on their own or in small groups, traipsing about in a disorganised rabble. It was not the British army's finest hour. A few vehicles went by – a lorry, a couple of jeeps, a staff car – and Joseph had conversations about taking his disabled companion on board. He got nowhere, and in any case Arthur was reluctant to see them separated.

'You're always better off with a mate,' he explained. 'I should know. A Don R is on his tod most of the time. I've enjoyed the last few days, even with a joker like you.'

'Surely the army looks after its wounded,' Joseph murmured.

'Yeah, it puts 'em in hospital. I don't want to spend years in a prisoner-of-war camp, thanks very much. I want to get on a boat.'

'I'll get you on a boat,' said Joseph.

A consequence of travelling amongst greater numbers was that they attracted the attention of the Luftwaffe. Raids by fighters and bombers sent men rushing for the ditches and hedgerows. There were inevitable casualties, with vehicles prominent amongst them – another reason why Arthur preferred sticking to the bike.

An advantage of the terrain south of Dunkirk was its unsuitability for German tanks. The pair went through mile after mile of marshy fields, criss-crossed by dykes, ditches and canals. Arthur pointed out one makeshift tank block – an old cart, a plough, some pieces of furniture –

but in general the abundance of water had kept the panzer divisions away. It was an asset in other ways too. A standard tactic for retreating British companies was to dig in behind a canal overnight and hold off the Germans during the day.

That night the two men slept under a hedge, as Arthur had predicted they would. It didn't rain, but if it had done they'd have got wet, along with hundreds of others. They were hungry, but better off than most of the troops, who'd been on half-rations since May 23rd. They were concerned about the bike – which would have been a find for some light-fingered compatriot – so, unsure of Lag's qualities as a lookout, Joseph lashed its frame to his thigh. His shoulder muscles ached from the unnatural exercise of bike-pushing and the ground beneath him was uneven, yet he was asleep within minutes of measuring his length; not before Arthur, though, who began snoring the moment his head touched the ground. Lag settled between them, receiving and bestowing warmth in roughly equal measures.

In the morning the cold ground held no attractions, and they were on the move by 6am. They'd have killed for a cup of tea but that was out of the question. They joined the hordes of soldiers who drifted in somnambulist fashion through the misty landscape. Wounded men were a common sight, helped on their way by makeshift crutches and other expedients. Arthur's bike was admired and coveted. A strapping sergeant tried to seize it off him but Lag – revealing unlooked for aggression – leapt forward to bury his teeth in the man's leg.

'You want to keep that hound under control,' barked the sergeant, in hasty retreat.

'Yes *sir*!' Arthur added insult to injury with a flaky salute, and called after the man 'I'm a bit concerned he might be rabid. Better get yourself checked out in Dunkirk.'

Animals formed an unexpected feature of the migration north. Dogs were two-a-penny, usually in the company of soldiers, but other beasts travelled unattached, seeking sustenance after finding themselves abandoned, or attracted to the notion of companionship. Joseph saw several goats, a small pig, and an unusually sociable sheep. A few cats kept clear of the melee and crept along the hedgerows. Doubtless all these creatures were fortunate to find troops on the move, or they'd have ended up on a spit over a roaring fire.

The strangest sight concerned two privates who'd tried to travel on a piebald mare found in a field. They'd no saddle or reins but had passed some rope through her mouth to serve as a crude bit. Somehow the men had got onto her back, though the one at the tail end was facing the wrong way. The unfortunate animal had been compliant till she realised neither man had a grasp of the equestrian arts, at which point she broke into a canter. There was cheering from the road as one rider slipped off the tail end and his mate went over the mare's head into a hedge. The incident raised the morale of all who saw it.

Even so, this was the longest day Joseph had known in his life. It was worse still for Arthur, whose leg caused constant pain, but they'd agreed to keep moving throughout daylight hours – and the night if necessary – until Dunkirk was reached. Twice they stopped to rest and watch the throng swarm past, but soon felt compelled to rejoin the exodus, to Lag's evident relief.

The light began to fail around 8pm. They knew Dunkirk was near because the flames were visible, like a beacon drawing men in. The crush of troops, like a single Leviathan creature, moved at a funereal pace. It was as well, because the road surface was disfigured by shell-holes which only became evident as men stumbled into them. By now any remaining vehicles were being driven away into the fields. Only the ambulances persisted, edging forward on the clutch – desperate affairs scored by bullets and shell fragments, windscreens thick with dust. They saw one of the drivers fall asleep at the wheel, so that the vehicle lurched forward, received with warning cries by the foot-sloggers around it. Joseph no longer tried to urge his companion into one of these ambulances. Arthur had developed a morbid fear of doctors, suspecting that a soldier who was absorbed into their medical bureaucracy could never extricate himself. 'Keep your options open' was his motto – no doubt echoed by every Don R in the service. 'I'll stay with you, Jos,' he would say. 'You're my lucky star.'

It was a melancholy aspect of the last few miles into Dunkirk that the the land on either side of the road was carpeted with these defunct vehicles: lorries, Jeeps, staff cars, motor-cycles, Bren gun carriers – every conceivable form of army machine lying smashed and abandoned. They saw parties of soldiers deployed to execute these tasks of destruction. Men drained vehicles of oil and water and left the engines running till they seized up, took sledge-hammers to bodywork and windscreens, and slashed tyres into pieces, operating – all too often – with a kind of insane energy. The canals and rivers were clogged with vehicles, sometimes so many that they were piled on top of each other. Of course Arthur recoiled from any damage to motor-cycles, but both men were horrified by the orgy of waste, the wholesale loss of an army's transport, annihilated in ways that affected the surrounding landscape. They found it hard to imagine the British army could be functional again in the years that lay immediately ahead.

At a point close to the town of Dunkirk, Arthur's bike became one more machine consigned to the military graveyard. Soldiers who arrived at that point were loaded into lorries and driven the last part of the journey, past the checkpoints keeping the Germans out, over one of the few bridges that had survived elimination. Joseph urged these troops to let Arthur's bike onto their lorry, but they were in no mood to mess about and argued (which turned out to be true) that a bike was unusable on Dunkirk's roads. So Arthur sat on the floor of the lorry, gazing at the filthy boots and bleeding feet of men who had tramped for days without being able to wash (and smelt like it). The mood of fear and uncertainty amongst the newcomers was palpable.

On arrival the men were shunted from the lorry without ceremony, finding themselves in what had once been a street. The driver pointed into the darkness saying 'The beach is that way', like a holiday guide shepherding tourists through a Cornish resort. After that they were on their own.

The problem of Arthur's mobility came to the fore again. The streets would indeed have been useless for a bicycle and were trial enough for men who were fully fit. The ground was littered with rubble and broken glass that crunched under-foot. A thick smoke swirled in the atmosphere and subjected the residents to fits of coughing. Joseph saw the body of a dead soldier slumped against a wall in an attitude of prayer. The only light came from buildings burning in the next road. Lag, who had never seemed bothered by anything, was unhappy, skulking tail down at the perimeters of the street.

'Wait there, mate,' Joseph told Arthur.

He approached a broken-down fence and ripped off a length of stanchion to serve as a crutch. With that in hand and Joseph's arm around him Arthur made crab-like progress. Both men stared wonderingly around this town, which had been a chimera for rootless troops when they were on the march, and now received them as a hopeless inferno. The street they were in featured a row of up-market shops. Most of these had been violently looted, but a couple of shop-fronts remained intact, striking a quaint note. In one, devoted to wedding dresses, a mannequin dressed in frilly splendour stared through its plate glass window at the inexplicable scenes in the road outside.

Their companions from the lorry-load of troops had magically dispersed, so Joseph and Arthur limped along an almost empty thoroughfare. Joseph became suddenly aware that the deep-seated booms which resounded permanently from the harbour area had been supplemented by a volley of sharper reports near to hand.

'That's small arms fire, isn't it?' he shouted.

'You're right,' said Arthur, 'Not at us, luckily. I think troops in the buildings opposite are exchanging fire with soldiers above us.' He indicated the storeys above the wedding shop. 'Which suggests, when you think about it, that some Germans have got inside the town.'

As he spoke a bullet pierced the window of the shop, sparking a clatter of falling glass.

'Time to make ourselves scarce,' said Arthur.

A front door opened nearby and they moved towards it. A woman in her 50s emerged and stood staring up towards the source of the shooting. She looked bemused rather than afraid, with a jaunty little smile playing around her lips.

Arthur swooped towards her, as quickly as his crutch allowed. 'You need to get off the street, lady. In there...' Then, '*Dedans...un coup de revolver*,' as the words magically came to him.

Still smiling she stood aside to motion them into the building, with no suggestion of haste. The two men exchanged a look but they obeyed, and Lag wasn't slow to follow.

The interior was unlit, though flames from burning buildings provided a flickering light to ease their way. Clearly, they were in an apartment block. A staircase led to the upper floors, with entrances to ground floor flats on either side, and the woman motioned them through one of these. They came to a small kitchen lit by an oil lamp, which shed light upon a wooden table and a stove fed by calor gas. They were in a downbeat part of town but the room was clean enough, considering what lay outside.

The woman gave her bright smile and signalled them to sit at table, then filled a kettle from a big saucepan of water and lit the gas under it. She also put down a saucer of water for Lag. It was only next day that they realised the extent of her sacrifice, surrendering water in a town that had no supplies of that essential commodity. What they appreciated at the time was her unwrapping a small packet of cheese, which she put on a plate next to some biscuits. When she left the room for a moment, moving in her strange, automaton-like way, Arthur couldn't restrain himself.

'*Cheese* – I love cheese.'

'But, d'you think we should?' whispered Joseph. 'I mean, is she...you know, all right...do you think?'

'A sandwich short of a picnic,' rejoined Arthur. 'But, still...cheese.'

'There's only one thing for it.' Joseph, fiddled in what had been their saddle-bag. 'We've got to give her some of the ham that's left.'

'Agreed, my friend. Exchange is no robbery.'

Back she came to make the tea. She nodded when Joseph indicated the ham, but nothing more. They sat together and ate the ham and cheese, and drank the tea. The men gave their names but couldn't extract an intelligible one from her.

Arthur ate leaning back against the wall. As they finished he started to fall asleep, head lolling to one side. Joseph supposed it was the most comfortable place he'd had for shut-eye in a couple of days. As with everything that happened the woman took it in her stride, showing no sign of surprise or annoyance. Joseph was desperate to take a leak, and muttered the word 'Toilet'. Again she nodded, escorting him to the door and pointing down the passage. He felt his way along it in near darkness, eventually pushing on a door that seemed the likely one. It was still dark within, but then a great burst of noise and light came through the window, illuminating the toilet bowl with the cistern behind it, and a bulky man on the seat with his trousers round his ankles. The blank, open eyes left no doubt at all that he was dead.

It seemed odd later, but in the moment Joseph's greatest need was to piss, and not in his own pants. He lumbered on down the passage, pushed at another door and found himself in the back garden, an unkempt area in which all kinds of weeds had run riot. In passing he wondered why their hostess was behaving with such unaffected kindness when a dead man, quite probably her husband, had been left sitting on the flat's toilet. It was something he really didn't want to dwell upon.

He was distracted by sounds coming from a neighbouring building, a house that lay immediately beyond a low garden fence. Someone was playing a piano, and the delicate strains were so clear that it seemed to be happening in the open air. Gazing across the fence he saw that the instrument had been pushed onto the veranda of the house and a young woman in evening dress sat at the keys. As he watched, her face was lit up by one of the many explosions that decorated the night sky. The limpid sound of her playing competed with the crash of detonations and the splutter of Joseph's piss as it plunged into the undergrowth. He knew the work that was being played. It was a Mozart 'Fantasie', a short piece written to precede the great C minor sonata, but sometimes said to overpower that work through its own powers of brilliant invention. As he listened Joseph found that tears were running down his face to drip into the earth he stood on.

Back indoors, Joseph was startled by a uniformed man who came bounding down the staircase – a hefty bloke who gave vent to his own exclamation of surprise.

'Bloody hell, I nearly gave you one there.' He brandished his rifle. 'What are you doing lurking about in the dark?'

Joseph briefly explained his situation with their unpredictable hostess.

'Bob Tennant, Coldstream Guards,' the bloke announced himself.

'We're having a bit of a barney with some Krauts in the building opposite. Seems they got across the canal on inflatables. So is your lady OK?'

'Actually I don't think she is. I wonder if you could give me a hand with something?'

'I shouldn't think so.'

Joseph told him about the corpse in the toilet.

'That's different,' said Tennant. 'Come on then.'

The Coldstream Guard could almost have handled the dead man single-handed. He lifted the body off the seat while Joseph adjusted the trousers to confer respectability. Together they hauled the dead weight into the back garden. There was a bit of tarpaulin lying in the undergrowth and they dragged it over the grim apparition.

'That'll have to do,' said Tennant. He cocked his head to take in the piano, still sending Mozart cascading into the night. 'Amazed anyone's got time for that belly-ache racket with everything else going on.'

'Someone trying to lead a normal life,' observed Joseph. 'Are a lot of locals still in town, do you think?'

'You'd be surprised, mate. On the other hand – if you think about it – where would they go to? Whole country's swarming with Germans. People want to die in their own back yard. Better than copping it on the open road, dragging a handful of belongings on your back. Either way, this sort of caper can send folks over the edge. Like your lady, poor devil.' He turned to go back inside. 'What about you? You free to leave?'

'Free as a bird.'

'Then get out quick as you can. Wait the night out here, then go down to the beach at first light. I'd say you've got two days max before the shutters come down.'

'And what about you?' Joseph asked.

Tennant shook his head. 'Oh no – we're for the high jump.'

Joseph went back inside, laid his head down on the kitchen table, and woke up seven hours later. He shook Arthur, who was still asleep in the previous evening's posture. Then Joseph started to worry, because his mate was less coherent than usual and seemed to be running a temperature. The woman materialised from somewhere – he never did know where – and he tried to convey their gratitude without ever being sure he'd got through to her. Dissatisfied, but anxious to get on, Joseph wrote down his name and address on a scrap of paper, and reiterated their thanks. It was as much as he could do.

They didn't make the beach by 'first light', as the Coldstream bloke had suggested, but were there before nine. Arthur's condition was a problem. In his rambling state of mind he couldn't handle the makeshift crutch. Joseph returned to the back garden and collected a wheelbarrow he'd spotted the previous evening, and they set off for the beach with that. It was quieter now, with no gunfire racketing between the buildings. Arthur put up no objections to the new mode of travel, and sat back in the barrow singing 'Pack up your troubles in your old kitbag'. A cat fled from the scene. A building damaged by shell-fire subsided gently into rubble amidst a haze of dust.

There was some relief in leaving behind the shell-shocked, no-man's-land of the town, passing through the dunes (with some difficulty on one wheel), and emerging onto the broad swathe of sandy beach as the ocean chuntered peacefully onto it and hundreds of men milled about. But with the sky congested by black smoke from burning oil tanks and a backdrop of fiercely burning buildings behind the dunes, this was a far cry from the beach holidays of Joseph's childhood.

Arthur might have been unaware of the singular circumstances, interrupting his singing to remark 'Should've brought my bucket and spade.'

'Arthur, I'm worried about you.' Joseph relinquished the wheelbarrow handles and knelt on the sand. 'Are you in much pain?'

'Where there's a Lucifer to light your fag,' the invalid sang, 'Smile boys that's the style.'

Joseph felt helpless, responsible for another human being who needed medical attention – urgently, in all probability – but with no idea what action to take. He was one amongst thousands in a similar position. The army was about following orders, but Dunkirk was unprecedented. Men had to make their own decisions, choosing in ignorance between life and death.

A soldier walked past grinning at Arthur. 'Your friend seems happy.'

'He's not himself,' said Joseph. 'He's hurt bad. Look, have you any idea what's going on?'

'What am I – the oracle? We're all in the dark here, mate.'

'I need to get this song-bird onto a boat.'

'You and thousands of others.'

'Yes but...what are the choices? Give me a clue, will you.'

The man took pity on him. 'Look, you can't go straight ahead, can you, though I've seen blokes do it – walk into the waves and drown themselves, drink sea-water, ugh! So you've only two choices, left or right. Go left and you'll reach the harbour. See that long wall reaching out into the sea?'

'Yes.'

'There are big ships moored in there, taking hundreds of troops on board. Don't know how you'd fare with the wheelbarrow, though. And the Krauts are shelling the harbour like crazy.'

'And if we go right?'

'There's eight miles of beach still in Allied hands – just about. And more big ships lying off the coast. Look, you can see 'em. Men queue on the beach, get picked up by the little boats, get taken out there.'

'No shelling of the beaches, then?'

'No shelling, but plenty of bombing and machine-gunning. That's when the queues scatter to the dunes and form up again afterwards. It's no picnic.'

'Thanks for the intelligence. One more thing. How long d'you reckon it takes to get on one of these little boats?'

'Don't know, mate, but I've been here 48 hours.'

Joseph gave him a look. 'OK. Thanks for your help.'

He and the wheelbarrow turned right, for no good reason other than a preference for wide open spaces.

The sight of the beaches – their sole objective for so many days – was a shock to the system; so many men scattered on the sands, it seemed barely possible they could all be picked up. One long queue of them curled back from the shallows, with the leaders in water up to their waists. Joseph recoiled from the thought of of exposing Arthur's injured leg to salt water. For that matter, many of the troops weren't queuing at all. He saw soldiers shaving, reading books, sleeping, making fires to brew up tea. An impromptu game of football was under way, using a bundle of clothing as a ball. Several men knelt to pray at the edge of the dunes, and further down the beach he could see a chaplain conducting a service. Other troops opted for more secular activities, like betting on which of the buildings along the Dunkirk skyline would be next to cop a German shell.

What really shocked him was the lack of boats. There were plenty in sight all right, but none that could be considered remotely functional. The wrecked hulls of small boats lurked half-submerged in the shallows, and dinghies, rowing-boats, motor-boats were stranded on the sands, amongst them the motor lifeboat *Mary Scott*, abandoned for an unknown reason. Amongst these vessels a few blue, bloated corpses lolled in the sea. A horrible smell lingered, the residue of death and destruction.

Without consciously forming a plan Joseph began moving down the beach, away from the harbour. At the back of his mind was the thought that, here amongst so many other men, they stood little chance of being picked up quickly. He worried that Arthur – now, improbably, sleeping in the barrow – needed urgent medical attention. Joseph knew that just two of them together stood a better chance, yet part of him yearned for company, for a unit to belong to. He remembered how alone he'd felt before he and Arthur had met so fortuitously, and realised how much he was missing the man's chirpy companionship. He even missed being called 'Jos'.

He pushed on down the beach, seeking out firm sand for the barrow's single wheel, wondering how long his wrists could tolerate the strain of their unnatural activity. The sight of a doctor or nurse would have been cause for celebration, but the army's medical services had gone missing. His thoughts wandered briefly to their distracted hostess in Dunkirk and what she'd have been doing since their departure.

A few hundred yards down the beach, where troop numbers had thinned out, the dunes gave way to a concrete promenade, then to the remains of what in better times had been a holiday resort. There was less bomb damage here but the buildings had an untended, sullen appearance. He passed a couple of sacked cafés, a bandstand, the outline of a cinema. The once-bright colours seemed unbecoming beside the spectacle of misery on the sands. He passed on as quickly as his ungainly contraption would allow. Lag scampered beside them.

After that Joseph came across a far more affecting sight. A kind of quay was set up at the water's edge, constructed from pontoons, and this had been become a resting place for wounded men – in theory waiting for boats, though none appeared on the horizon. The injuries must have been serious, or the men concerned would have got up and walked away. They suffered quietly, but there were inevitable groans and cries and pleas for water, so that a restrained clamour issued from the pier to drift across the empty sands. A couple of chaplains stood by, doing their best for the men. Otherwise these unfortunates had been left to their fate. Lag barked at the sight of them and the hairs stood up on the back of his neck.

A single able-bodied man, a corporal, was standing near the pier as Joseph went by.

'Depressing bloody sight, isn't it?' the man said.

'How long have they been there?' asked Joseph.

'Too long. The boats won't pick 'em up.'

'Oh?'

Well...they might, but then the big ships won't take them on board. They've got orders to accept fit men first. The wounded use up too much room on deck.'

'That's not very nice.'

'You're telling me?'

For a while Arthur had appeared to be asleep in the barrow, or unconscious, but now he sat up and raised his head, sniffing the air, listening to the doleful choir coming from the quay. Some sort of connection with his own condition asserted itself for he abruptly went berserk, howling guttural, unreadable cries, throwing himself from the wheelbarrow to crawl several yards along the sand.

The corporal helped Joseph put him back again. 'Give him some water,' he said.

'I don't have any.'

'It's water he needs.' The corporal looked at the wounded on the quay, then back at Arthur. 'Get him out of here. Get him on a boat.'

Further on an opportunity for water presented itself. Half-a-dozen soldiers stood behind some wooden crates, watching over various items displayed on top of them.

'What's going on here?' said Joseph. 'I need water. My friend's in a bad way.'

'We might be able to help, sort of,' said a man with a bandaged arm. 'But you'll have to barter for it.'

Joseph reacted furiously. 'I don't believe this. Surely you're not trying to make a profit out of the desperate men on this beach?'

'Calm down, soldier,' said bandaged-arm. 'Nobody profits out here, haven't you noticed? We offer a service. There *is* no water in Dunkirk. We've got thousands of thirsty men on the beaches. What can you offer instead?'

Joseph calmed down. The man seemed reasonable enough once he started talking. 'All I've got is some ham, and not much of that.'

'That'll do it. What we have isn't exactly water, mind you. This crate contains tins of boiled potatoes in a fluid.'

'Oh! So what does it taste like?'

'It's revolting. Let me see the ham.'

Joseph handed over the pathetic remains of their ham, and the soldier signalled to his mate for a tin of potatoes. Someone punctured it with a bayonet through the lid. Joseph helped Arthur to drink, trying to avoid spillage. Arthur only stopped when all the liquid had gone.

'What else have you got there?' said bandaged-arm.

Joseph shook his head. 'We're right out. Thanks anyway.'

'Here.' The soldier opened another tin and handed it over.

'Thank you. I appreciate that. Thanks a lot.' Joseph took a swig then stepped back, retching from the greasy flavour. 'It's vile.'

'Told you.'

He drank what he could and poured some into Lag's mouth.

In the early afternoon Joseph felt he could push the wheelbarrow no further, and joined one of the queues. A long file of men straggled back from a pier formed by lorries driven into the sea. Their subdued mood was easy to understand. Occasional boats turned up to carry troops away but more soldiers were constantly arriving, so the queue never shortened. It also received the attentions of the Luftwaffe. On his own with the wheelbarrow, Joseph had found he was untroubled by air attacks, but once a body of men gathered together they attracted the German pilots. Between mid-afternoon and dusk there were three waves of of them. Men scattered onto the dunes but there were still casualties. When the planes had dispersed the queue reformed, after a fashion, with much pushing and shoving and arguing. It was a soul-destroying business. With Arthur in such dire straits Joseph didn't even try to move, instead sheltering them both under the barrow during each blitz. Some clangs on the metal frame showed that the wheelbarrow had its uses. Other men half-buried themselves in the sand, forming rudimentary slit trenches that absorbed the shock from bombs. None of these measures guaranteed safety, as evidenced by the sprinkling of little wooden crosses scattered around the beach.

As the afternoon wore on it was clearly unlikely that men queueing there would be picked up in the near future, yet Joseph stayed where he was. During the day – or perhaps earlier – the iron had entered his soul. Not that he was fevered like Arthur, but he was worn down, weary from foot-slogging, mentally shot from making decisions for the pair of them. His wrists were inflamed from constantly pushing at the cumbersome wheelbarrow. He rested his head on the damp sand and dozed, feeling the reassurance of Lag's body against his. Arthur murmured from the barrow. Men all around slept, surrendering to the comforting presence of companions. As the night grew chilly Joseph pulled his great-coat closer.

The sky darkened and the surface of the sea took on a glassy quality. The noise of the surf was a soothing presence. Once Joseph heard the sound of oars and raised his head to see the outline of a boat. There were splashes and murmurs of encouragement as men got hauled aboard. A luminous phosphorescence bathed the whole scene, giving a ghostly air to every rope, every footstep in the sand, the edge of every wave. At another time in another place he'd have been dazzled by it.

He woke a second time to the sound of Lag whining. The dog was on its hind legs, front paws on the barrow, licking Arthur's face. Joseph touched his friend's forehead, which was much too hot. The man was rambling in his sleep, a torrent of half intelligible words, about being in a sanatorium, about a brother in danger, about a church with a stained glass window. References to his mother were so frequent it almost seemed he'd reverted to his youth, and twice he spoke with a childllike intonation. Much of what he said seemed to be nonsense, especially the repeated phrase "There's plenty of five at the dime-and-five". His voice rose so high that men stirred from sleep and turned blearily towards the disturbance. One of them was conscious enough to address Joseph.

'You know there's a hospital.'

'What?'

'Yeah. Down the beach. Not far.'

'A hospital! Are you sure about this?'

'No kidding,' said the soldier, relapsing into sleep.

Joseph got to his knees, then onto his feet. 'Come on, Lag,' he said. Pain racked his fore-arms as he took hold once more of the wretched wheelbarrow. A gleam of light on the horizon told him that dawn was on its way. He trudged forward again, from obstinacy rather than any sense of hope. At least Arthur was quietened by the movement. The sound of surf was constant as the barrow's wheel squeaked along the sand. There was no-one else about.

The light was still murky when Joseph heard an unusual hammering sound, distant at first but moving steadily closer. A confused blur came out of the gloom and swept past him in a fury of sound and movement that had Lag barking like crazy. For a second he saw the frenetic, galloping forms of several horses, then they were gone. When he thought about this later it seemed likely the animals had been abandoned by French artillery units.

Joseph pressed blindly on until the eternal dunes gave way to a great, heavy building that loomed up austerely against the sea and sands. There was a sign, 'Zuydcoote Maritime Hospital'. A hospital! *The* hospital! Not a mirage or the product of a fevered soldier's brain, but a real, actual hospital. He could scarcely believe his luck.

He took the wheelbarrow through the main entrance with Lag loping behind and was swallowed up by the vastness of the place. Because it was so dark inside, Joseph felt he'd entered a massive tomb. At the far end of a hall the size of a small football pitch a woman in nun's habit was just about visible, standing beside an oil lamp.

'*Les chiens son prohibees*,' she said as they approached.

'I'm so sorry,' said Joseph. 'I can't speak French.'

She smiled and continued in serviceable English. 'No, it is *me* who is sorry. It was a silly joke about the dog. How can I help?'

He indicated the wheelbarrow and explained about Arthur's injury. 'My friend has been babbling all night. I'm really worried about him.'

She took Arthur's temperature and felt his pulse, then got Joseph to hold the oil lamp over the wounded leg.

'I am afraid this does not look good,' she said eventually.

Joseph had already formed the impression that she was a woman to be trusted. 'What should I do?' he said. 'Can the hospital help him?'

'I will say the truth,' she told him. 'We do what we can here. Many doctors they have gone away, but the nuns try to help. We are the Sisters of Mercy. The hospital, he does not have every equipment he need and not every medicine also. And many men they come here and need treatment. Too many men.' She pointed across the hall to a stretcher case that had just come through the main entrance in an urgent flurry of noise.

'Please tell me what I should do,' Joseph repeated.

The nun looked at him very directly. 'If you can, take him home on a boat. He will have better chance in an English hospital. After 24 hours and no boat, come to us and we shall try to help.'

Joseph nodded, albeit with reluctance. The weight of responsibility, so briefly offloaded, had surged back onto his own head. But the nun's advice was clear enough and he knew now what to do, though with little idea how to do it. He thanked her.

'I will bring pills for his pain,' she said. 'Please wait here – it will be five minutes.' She made a walking motion to indicate that the medicines were some distance away.

'I understand,' Joseph said. 'This hospital is a very big place.'

She smiled. 'It is lucky that people call Sisters of Mercy "The walking nuns". Do you have enough water?'

He shook his head. 'Nobody has water.'

'We have. This we do have.' She pointed. 'Look over there.'

In the corner of the vast entrance hall was a standpipe, which seemed like a mirage. He filled his water bottle and Arthur's, while Lag lapped up liquid that had splashed to the ground beneath.

A little later – it was more like ten minutes – he was pushing Arthur out of the hospital and back onto the sandy beach. As he did so the wheel of the barrow lurched sideways and broke away, beyond fixing even by an engineer. Joseph cursed but at the same time felt a certain sense of relief, aware that he was physically unable to shove the wretched thing any further; he was all but done in. He sat down on the sand and gazed at the sea - waves that came, waves that went – longing for a boat to materialise but knowing it wouldn't. It didn't occur to him to pray because he no longer believed in miracles, if he ever had. Joseph wasn't one for introspection, or he might have concluded that he was in despair.

'You OK, chum?'

He looked up to find a young man in sailor's uniform standing beside him.

'Not exactly.' He explained about Arthur and the hospital, and the broken wheelbarrow, and the need to get picked up by a boat.

'You know, there's a beached motor-boat not far from here,' the sailor said. '*Malden Annie IV*, she's called. I passed there ten minutes ago and she was a few yards out in the shallows. Could be ideal for getting picked up.'

Joseph stared at him.

'Come on,' said the young man. 'You never know your luck.' He held a hand out. 'Leading Seaman Vic Viner. They call me a beach-master. No, don't ask. Let's get your friend out of this barrow and along to *Malden Annie*. You take one arm and I'll do the other. We'll soon get him there, don't you worry.'

~ Six ~

The transfer of Joseph and Arthur from *Malden Annie IV* to *Blithe Spirit* was accomplished with little fuss. Mr Sellick claimed not to have noticed there was a dog as well as the two men, but at no time did they consider leaving Lag behind. In fact Mr Sellick liked dogs, and so – it transpired – did most of the troops in the cabin, where Joseph and Arthur were installed. With 17 men there now and another ten up on deck, *Blithe Spirit* sat low in the water; no more so than when she'd been off-loading soldiers onto destroyers but this was different, for she faced a five-hour journey to Ramsgate across the open sea.

Mr Sellick took her back past the harbour, giving a wide berth to the entrance so as to keep clear of the big ships manoeuvring in and out. He cast an anxious eye at the sky. It was 09.30 in the morning and the low cloud that had been their welcome companion through most of the voyage had inconveniently given way to bright sunlight. Once away from the harbour area, where burning oil tanks still belched black smoke into the sky, they were a sitting target for any German pilots who cared to give them the once-over. He could only hope that the Luftwaffe, if they showed up, would consider a measly motor-boat too insignificant to waste time on.

Initially Mr Sellick and Tyler kept to the wheel-house while Chrissie circulated amongst the troops. She took along the first aid box and a pitcher of water, but most of the men went out like a light the moment they came on board. She felt weary enough to join them, yet knew that her fifteen hour shift was a bagatelle when set against the days men had spent tramping the well-worn roads to Dunkirk.

The cabin was crammed with bodies sprawled across every inch of space. Troops slept tangled up in curious juxtapositions, oblivious to every external factor. The poky quarters pullulated with snores, grunts and laboured breathing. Arthur dozed in a corner while Joseph, sitting beside him, told Chrissie what the Sister of Mercy had said in the hospital. She managed to raise the level of Arthur's wounded leg, as nurses were advised to do, but could suggest little else to improve his condition.

'How long has your friend been like this?' she asked.

'Forty-eight hours plus,' Joseph told her. 'He'll be all right, won't he?'

'We must get him to the doctors in Ramsgate as soon as possible,' Chrissie prevaricated. She didn't like the smell coming off Arthur's wound – and this in a cabin that stank to high heaven, sardine-packed with men who hadn't washed for days. In her brief experience there'd been a wound that smelt suspiciously like Arthur's once before, but Chrissie hoped she was wrong about that.

'He's a good man,' said Joseph. 'He deserves to be OK.' Then abruptly changing tack, he asked 'Is there anything I can do to help you?'

Chrissie was touched by his enquiry, unusual amongst these bone-weary men. She told him 'Thanks, but you get some sleep yourself.'

'I'm an engineer by the way,' Joseph said. 'You never know, it may come in useful.' He cocked his head, listening. 'Though your engine sounds pretty good at the moment.'

'I appreciate the offer,' she said. 'Let's hope we don't need to use it.'

She rejoined her father and Tyler in the wheel-house and for a time followed with often horrified attention the progress of other ships using Route X. The traffic far exceeded anything they'd seen on their own voyage out. Small boats were mostly unscathed, but with the larger ships Mr Sellick's fears about bombers operating in cloudless skies were sadly vindicated. As a case in point they were passed by the destroyer *Scimitar* and the mine-sweepers *Halcyon* and *Queen of Thanet*, all crammed with French troops, only to discover later that these men had been taken off the stricken steamer *Prague*.

What really brought home the futility of war was the sight of the *Ivanhoe*, severely damaged, being assisted by another tug; yes the *Ivanhoe*, to which they'd delivered several batches of soldiers in their own minuscule contribution to the war effort. But now the destroyer's decks showed no sign of troops, who'd been off-loaded onto other vessels. It needed little thought to conclude that some of the men who'd been in *Blithe Spirit's* cabin earlier that morning, exhilarated by their deliverance from the beaches, had been killed or wounded on the deck of the *Ivanhoe*. Such reflections made Chrissie ashamed of her prior excitement at the sight of conflict. She brooded about the men drowned or blasted to pieces or badly injured, and the grief of their friends and relatives; and the ridiculous wholesale destruction of so much shipping, when she was obsessed by a single, ancient motor yacht that could be blown out of the sea at any moment.

Her gloomy ruminations weren't redeemed when *Blithe Spirit* passed the remains of the 3,500-ton transport ship, *Scotia*, sinking stern first with her forward funnel and mast under water.

Ninety minutes out of Dunkirk Mr Sellick's fears of an attack were realised, when they were machine-gunned by several Messerschmidts. The assault was ineffective because the German pilots curiously elected to stay at 2,000 feet, though this did little to reassure the nervous men on the top deck, who were directly in the line of fire. After 20 minutes three Hurricanes came on the scene and the Germans made themselves scarce, pursued by ribald cheers from British troops above and below *Blithe Spirit's* decks.

This was one of the rare occasions when the Royal Air Force effort at Dunkirk was actually witnessed by British troops, and it helped to offset the opinion – widely held – that British fliers had left their army colleagues out to dry. By coincidence they soon saw a different aspect of RAF activity, when Tyler spotted white parachute nylon spread on the waves some distance to starboard. It belonged to a Hurricane pilot who'd bailed out when his plane took multiple hits from German fighters. He'd delayed pulling the ripcord as long as possible whilst personally under fire, eventually coming down in the drink, where he was sustained by his life-jacket. The man was highly relieved when *Blithe Spirit* picked him up, and astonished by the cheers he got from British troops on board. He told Mr Sellick that a mate of his, who'd parachuted down near Dunkirk, hadn't been allowed onto a British minesweeper because of the RAF's perceived inertia.

Not long afterwards the thing Chrissie had feared ever since leaving Ramsgate actually happened, when one of *Blithe Spirit's* engines cut out. She cursed, then nodded to her father and went to lift up the deck boards above the offending engine. Luckily, the light was as good as it had been all trip, and she soon found the source of the trouble. Fixing it was another matter. As she crouched over the engine, spotlight in hand, Joseph materialised beside her.

'This is your fault,' she said. 'You said the engines were running well.'

'Sod's law,' he rejoined, unabashed. 'It's the copper piping, isn't it?'

She nodded. 'Broken free from the carburettor, damn it.'

'Still, the boat's done pretty well considering what you've had to put it through. Is it OK if I try and help?'

'Of course,' she said, a bit dubious because she knew so little about him.

He peered and prodded briefly. 'Copper's so brittle. There's always that risk, with all the vibration. Especially as you're so heavily loaded. You know, it helps to have a couple of spirals at the end of the pipe.'

'They're there - look.'

'Yes, but better if they're horizontal. A vertical loop makes a trap for dirt to form.'

'Interesting.' She was momentarily fascinated by the technical challenge, forgetting their situation in the English Channel.

'It's a good job you've got a drip tray underneath the carb,' he went on. 'Much safer.'

She looked at Joseph with new eyes as he bent over the engine, calm and quietly confident. 'You know what you're doing, don't you?'

He grinned. 'Don't sound so surprised.'

'I'm just grateful.'

'We're going to need a new joint,' he said. 'Look, I think I could bodge up some sort of cone union, with your help, if you've got the basic tools.'

'Of course. I'm a mechanic, don't you know. But mainly on cars.'

'Come on then, let's have a go.'

She went to tell her father what was going on, and Mr Sellick said he'd make what progress he could on the other one.

For half an hour Joseph worked on the pipe, with Chrissie by his side handing over tools and holding things in place as instructed. She'd always made a point of watching how other mechanics worked – her father reckoned this marked her down for management – and was often able to see a better way of tackling any specific task. But watching Joseph at work, she was the one in learning mode. She admired the neat, unruffled way he approached each new challenge. She forgot her doubts about his abilities.

'I don't even know your name,' she said.

'It's Joseph. Although...'

'What?'

'No, it's a silly thing. My friend in the cabin – Arthur – he started calling me "Jos" and I got to quite like it. It happened after...well, it's a long story.'

'I don't mind long stories.'

They were closeted away from the others, and he felt the pull of interest in this stranger crouched beside him, but even so... 'It's not an incident I'm proud of,' he said. 'It went against everything I believe. Arthur said forget it, but I'm more straight-laced than him...'

'Well Jos,' she said, 'People can always change, can't they.'

His features coloured with embarrassment. 'Hold that pipe firmly in place,' he said. 'You're doing my head in.'

'That sounds promising.'

'Besides...I don't even know *your* name.'

'It's Chrissie...Jos'

Once they'd finished the repairs Joseph returned to Arthur's side. Chrissie signalled her father to restart the engine, and *Blithe Spirit* surged forward in the calm sea. The men on deck gave a ragged cheer; it was becoming a habit with them. As it turned out, the engine was fixed just in time, because soon afterwards the boat attracted the attention of a single Stuka – and this one showed no inclination to go away.

'He's going to dive,' said Mr Sellick. 'Chrissie, take the wheel and do exactly as I say.' He stood outside with his eyes fixed on the sky. In the wheel-house Chrissie heard the Stuka screaming towards them. Every instinct urged her to turn the wheel but she waited.

'Hard aport,' came her father's calm instruction.

She turned the wheel and *Blithe Spirit* responded. The bomb landed too close for comfort on the starboard side, sending water over the deck.

'A near thing,' said Mr Sellick. 'And we're going to do it again.'

Chrissie had always admired her father's mastery of steering and had never emulated him to her own satisfaction. She knew that when the wheel is turned hard to one side the boat takes a couple of lengths to respond. Getting it exactly right was a matter of fine judgement and in this situation, when one accurate bomb would send them all to the bottom of the channel, the stakes couldn't have been higher. No-one would have known it from Mr Sellick's demeanour, which suggested a weekend sailor on a casual trip down the coastline.

'Hard astarboard,' he remarked, in his conversational tone.

Chrissie responded and the bomb fell to port, further away this time. Again a cheer came from the men on deck. Troops in the cabin would have known little of what was happening; if a bomb did hit the mark they'd go down with the boat.

The German pilot made two more attempts, each time outwitted by the part-time English sailor below, then lost interest. Unfortunately he was replaced by another Stuka, which came in with the obvious intention of machine-gunning *Blithe Spirit* from bow to stern. Once again Mr Sellick gave his impassive instructions and bullets went harmlessly into the sea. Chrissie realised her father's demeanour was intended in part to reassure the men on deck, who were directly exposed to machine-gun fire. But as the Stuka came in again some of them lost confidence in the ducking-and-diving routine and began clambering down to get into the cabin. The distraction affected Mr Sellick's instructions and Chrissie's response to them. At the same time Tyler, knowing their onrush would throw the boat out of kilter, ran forward to hurl the men back, shouting 'Stay where you are'.

The sound – when it came – of the Stuka's bullets connecting with *Blithe Spirit* left Chrissie white with fright. A single line of holes scarred the planking and it was Tyler who'd intercepted them. He fell without a murmur at the entrance to the wheel-house. Despite herself, Chrissie cried out.

'Oh Tyler.'

The shock showed on Tyler's face but he made an effort to grin. 'Don't fret, Chrissie, it's an occupational hazard.' There was blood – too much of it – on the deck, and Tyler's trouser leg was soaked with the stuff.

Mr Sellick came quickly forward, serious-faced but unflappable. 'I'm sorry, lad. I hoped we'd get away with that.'

'You were brilliant, sir,' said Tyler.

'We'll get you into the cabin. You'll be comfortable there. You have a look at Tyler's leg Chrissie, won't you. Try and find a reliable man to keep an eye on him. You're going to be needed out here. Even more so now.'

'I know who'll look after him,' said Chrissie.

By good fortune the Stuka had called off the attack, no doubt unaware that his last sally had hit. Chrissie found two 'volunteers' from the cabin – they had to be woken up – to carry Tyler in to where Joseph sat. She followed with the first aid box. She took a knife and started cutting away Tyler's uniform at the thigh.

'Don't tell my girlfriend you're doing this,' Tyler murmured.

She forced a smile. 'I won't if you don't. Now Tyler, you need to stay nice and quiet. And *still*, once I've bound you up.'

One bullet had grazed his knee but a second – the serious one – was buried in the thigh. From the amount of blood, she thought it might have nicked the femoral artery. (They'd banged on about arteries at the Red Cross course.) Mr Sellick kept half a bottle of whisky in the first aid box and she poured some on the bullet's entry point and bound the thigh tightly.

She turned to Joseph. 'Would you mind...?'

'I'll keep an eye open,' Joseph assured her. 'Any problem, I'll give you a shout. Don't worry.'

'I won't – not if you're on it.'

'What do you think?' Mr Sellick asked when she returned to him.

'I don't know. It's only one bullet but...'

'A lot of blood.'

'I know.'

They stood side by side as *Blithe Spirit* plodded across the placid waters, with her motors beating out the regular rhythm every mariner needed to hear. The sun shone on the glassy surface. The troops on deck had returned shame-faced to their places and those in the cabin slept. It might have been just Chrissie and her father in the boat were it not for the heavy way it handled.

'So...this is war, girl,' Mr Sellick said out of nowhere. 'The real thing. Not so much fun, is it?'

She turned with a little cry of distress. 'I never said it was fun...'

'No, you didn't. You've done well. How are you feeling?'

'OK.' She shrugged. 'A bit strange, actually.'

'Hardly surprising. You've been nearly 24 hours on the go. Mental and physical strain of a sort you've never faced before.'

'Yes but what about you – you being so old and all!'

He cuffed her lightly round the ear. 'Now look, I reckon we're still three hours out of Ramsgate. We must both try to stay alert. You get some shut-eye while it's peaceful like this.' He pointed to the deck. 'Even an hour would do it – pep you up.'

'But I wouldn't get to sleep down there.'

'You'd be surprised. Try it. Just lie down and close your eyes.' He took off his thick sailing coat and laid it on the deck.

'But dad, you can't do that!' she cried. 'Remember what you always say about clothes. You have to feel "just right".'

'I'll give you "Just right", my girl. Lie down and for once in your life do as you're told.'

To Chrissie's great surprise her father was right. She remembered laying her head on the coat, then the next thing was sitting up to look round. It seemed that nothing had changed. Mr Sellick was still at the wheel and *Blithe Spirit* chugged across the Channel with water slapping at its sides. The sky was empty; nothing malignant in sight.

'Welcome back,' said her father.

'What – did I sleep?'

'An hour and a half.'

'Oh!' She scrambled to her feet.

'Would you check on Tyler?' he said.

'Of course.'

She entered the cabin with more water. The dog raised its head attentively, but Joseph was the only person awake. She warmed to him, that he'd made the effort. He shrugged when she looked enquiringly in Tyler's direction, pointing to the dark stain on deck.

'And what about your friend?' Chrissie said, remembering Arthur.

'He's delirious.' Joseph bent to dribble some water into Arthur's mouth. 'Comes out with all sorts of daft stuff, nursery rhymes and so on. Humpty Dumpty's in there somewhere. Keeps saying "There's plenty of five at the dime and five", over and over again.'

'What does it mean?'

'I've no idea.'

Tyler muttered something and opened his eyes.

'Aha!' said Chrissie. 'He speaks. How are you?'

'OK. A bit feeble.'

'I'm not surprised, with a bullet in your leg.'

She felt his forehead – which seemed cool enough – then took his pulse, which she didn't like at all.

Tyler said 'Will you do something for me?'

'Of course.'

'Have you got a pencil and paper?'

'No, but I can get some.'

'I want you to write a note to my girl-friend.'

Instinctively, she touched his arm. 'Tyler, come on – we're not in that territory. It's just one bullet. You'll be fine.'

'Good! If I am, then there's no harm done, eh?'

He held her gaze until she relented. 'Well all right, but just to keep you happy, you understand. Hold on a mo'.'

She went to fetch something to write with. On her return Joseph had fallen asleep, or tactfully pretended to. She brandished the pencil at Tyler and sat beside him.

'Fire away then. What's your girlfriend's name?'

He gave the girl's name and the address in Northampton, then dried up. Chrissie sat with pencil raised.

Tyler looked pale but reasonably in charge of his faculties. 'Don't rush me,' he said. 'It's difficult. I've not done it like this before.'

'Of course not. How often do you write usually?'

'Well...I haven't, really.'

'Huh! Typical male.'

She waited some more but nothing happened. She said 'Do you want me to suggest things she might like to hear?'

'Well, yes, maybe. If you think you could. What do you have in mind?'

'Dear Sandra, I'm lying on the deck of a small motor-boat with a bullet in my leg and I'm thinking of you.'

'Yes, that's good. I like that. Put that down.'

She wrote.

'What else?' said Tyler.

Chrissie bit the end of the pencil. It occurred to her that she'd never written anything along these lines, and had never wanted to either. What would it feel like to be Tyler? And if she were Sandra, what would *she* want to hear? She looked round the cabin, which was trembling with the sounds of men snorting and sleeping. Joseph – Jos – sat beside her, head resting against the wall, looking strangely innocent. She felt surprisingly good about having him there. She gazed at his face for a moment. 'When we're together I feel comfortable and right,' she said.

'You're so clever,' Tyler said.

'If only you knew,' she replied.

'Write it.'

She wrote.

'Please say more,' Tyler said.

'It's so hard with the war and all the coming and going, but I'd like to think we'll both feel the same when the fighting stops. I believe in you. You're honest and real and that's what counts for me.'

'You amaze me, Chrissie,' Tyler said. 'I didn't think anyone could understand what I felt. Write it.'

She wrote.

'Now you should say something about how you got the bullet,' she told him.

'Whoa.' In his agitation he tried to sit up. 'No, nothing like that. Definitely not. I think we've got enough now. Just let me sign it.' She gave him the pencil and held the paper but he couldn't manage to write. That was when she started really to worry about him. 'Never mind, just put my name,' he finished off.

'I don't know it, Tyler.'

'It's Charles.'

'Charles. OK.'

She added the name and said 'I'm going to put a note telling her who's writing this,' but Tyler's eyes had closed. 'I'll make sure she gets it,' she said.

For the first time since they'd left Dunkirk the men in the cabin showed signs of life. One woke, then another, and then they all followed suit. The congested space was crammed with soldiers stretching, coughing, spluttering, trying out the jokes that were inseparable from wartime life and made it bearable. Several men wrenched off boots to examine their feet, then wished they hadn't. There were urgent requests for water. Chrissie stood up and said she'd be back with a jug of the stuff.

In the wheel-house she told her father that Tyler's condition worried her. 'I don't know what else to do, dad.'

'You can't do anything, girl. Give the men something to drink, and whatever else they need if we've got it. The ones on deck too. I'll shout if I need you. Shouldn't be long now – I'd say we're less than an hour from Ramsgate.'

Chrissie also sensed their proximity to England. It was too hazy actually to see the coast but there were more gulls around. She wasn't sure what to feel about coming home. They'd been away less than 24 hours yet everything had changed. Her old life felt flat by comparison.

She saw to the troops on deck, then took water round the cabin. The atmosphere was a lot livelier. It got quite ribald after she made an announcement about *shedding* water 'outside, in the sea'. There were the usual jokes about having a female in their midst.

'It's a Dunkirk miracle, miss,' said the joker of the group. 'Three hundred thousand men – and you.'

'No, Albert – you're wrong there.' The joker was contradicted by a serious looking chap, slightly older than the rest. 'There's another woman on the *Dinard*.'

'Get away. You sure you're not thinking of the ship's figurehead.'

'No, honestly. It's a Mrs Goodrich. She was a stewardess when the *Dinard* did its cross-channel runs in peacetime and she's still on the job. I know a bloke who's seen her out there. No spring chicken, either. She's fifty-nine, he told me.'

'Oh well then. We'll stay with this young lady.'

'You don't have a choice,' Chrissie said.

She was used to being the lone female with men, but the idea of two amongst 300,000 was hard to get her head round. It was fantastic. What an absurd world we live in, she thought. She'd have liked to meet this Goodrich woman to compare notes. The pair of them were unique specimens – if two people could be described as unique.

As they neared the English coast other matters were aired in the confined cabin space. One of the men had mentioned a chaplain and Chrissie – ever her father's irreligious daughter – put in her sniffy two-penny's worth.

'I've never seen the point of chaplains on the battlefield. I mean, can they can actually do anything?'

'Oh yes, miss,' said the serious bloke. 'They do a lot.'

A murmur of assent came from others. 'It's not about religion,' said a second man. 'I'm no believer but I believe in chaplains all right. They're always the last to leave, you know.'

'That's right.' The joker, waved a hand around the cabin. 'Do you see any chaplains here, miss?'

'Well no.'

'There you go then. They're still out there – on the beaches. They're the only officers whose whole job is to look after us. To care for the men.'

'I'm sorry,' said Chrissie to the cabin at large. 'I didn't realise.'

'Don't you worry, miss,' said the serious man. 'You weren't to know. You're up there with the chaplains in our estimation.'

All the same Chrissie resolved, not for the first time, to think more before she spoke.

The subject that dominated the men's thoughts, and their conversation, was the reception they were about to receive in Britain. The nearer they got to the coast the more on edge troops became.

'I ain't looking forward to this,' someone said. 'Sooner it's over the better.'

'Me an' all,' said another. 'Don't forget, we're the blokes what've lost the war.'

'You were in Ramsgate before, miss,' said the serious man. 'What was it like when troops came back from France? Did you ever see it happen?'

'I did.' Chrissie was cautious after her thoughtless remark about chaplains, but decided to tell the truth. 'It was a bit depressing, I have to say. The men came back and us lot in the town just watched. Nobody said anything. You could've heard a pin drop.'

'It's not surprising,' someone else chipped in. 'We've lost the war. We've messed everything up. We can't go on blaming the bleedin' Froggies, pardon my French.'

'We can have a damn good try at *that*,' said the joker.

'Not even that. Think about it. We went out there, spent six months drinking their wine and sitting on our backsides, an' the first time someone takes a shot at us we come running back, tails between our legs.'

'An' half the navy is wiped out trying to get us out of there,' said a corporal.

'I still don't understand what happened. I keep thinking of all those people lining the streets when we went into Belgium. Shouting and cheering. I got kissed by the local women.'

'Don't expect kisses in Ramsgate,' said the corporal. 'I hope people say nowt, like miss says. Let'em just look and leave us alone. We done our best but it weren't good enough.'

The man who started all the miserable talk shivered and repeated his catch-phrase. 'Bloody hell, I ain't looking forward to this.'

Chrissie thought of offering to drop them all off on the Goodwin Sands, but decided she'd made enough uncouth remarks for one day. Mr Sellick called to her from the wheelhouse. She went up to join him and found they'd arrived. The familiar walls of Ramsgate harbour were almost on top of them. Through the entrance went *Blithe Spirit* and Chrissie gasped in surprise, for tied up along the harbour front were more boats than she'd ever seen, while the pavements above the harbour steps were seething with people. Ramsgate was alive and kicking. An excited clamour reached their ears across the water.

Mr Sellick throttled back the engines, which meant that within minutes *Blithe Spirit* herself would have berthed. Chrissie watched the quay rush upon them with a sense of panic, because something had unexpectedly become clear to her. She plucked at her father's sleeve, as she used to do when a little girl.

'Dad, there's something I want to say.'

'What is it, Chrissie?'

'I mean, we've finished this trip, I know, but the thing isn't over, is it?'

'What are you saying?'

She stumbled on. 'Thousands of men are still out there. What will happen to them?'

'Those that can't find a ship will be stuck on the sands, or in the harbour. The Germans will move in and make them prisoners of war. They'll have a bad time.'

'That's what I thought, so...' The words sounded strange as she said them. 'So I think we should go back.'

Sometimes she'd know from his expression what her father was thinking, but not now. 'You know we've been lucky this time,' he said at length. 'One life-threatening injury – it's hard on Ryder but that's a good result in a scene like Dunkirk. It's not likely we'd be as fortunate again.'

'I know that.'

'You're a young woman, Chrissie, with your life ahead of you.'

'I was thinking about how we'd feel if we *don't* go back...if we just went home. How would we feel then?'

He looked at her – a long, long look, as if he were considering what to do with his only daughter. Then 'You're right of course. You have that way with you – a way of getting the important things right.' He stooped to pick up a rope as *Blithe Spirit* bumped against the harbour side, and threw it to the waiting men. 'All right then. I'll have to see if there's a convoy going out this evening. And if they can find us a third man to replace Tyler.'

'And someone to check over the engines,' she said.

'And that's not all, is it? I'll have to talk to your mother. God alone knows what she'll say.'

'*God*, dad? Surely not.'

Mr Sellick stepped off the boat into the ferment of activity on the quay. The first person he saw was Malan.

'Still here?' he said. 'Well nobody could complain about the hours you land-lubbers are putting in.'

'Welcome back, Mr Sellick.' Malan was all brisk endeavour as usual. 'Is everything OK with your lot?'

'We've two injured men on board, one of them Tyler. He's in a bad way.' Malan was already beckoning forward stretcher-bearers and nurses. 'Listen Malan, we want to go back to Dunkirk, if you can find us a convoy. And we need a man to replace Tyler. You were right about that, by the way – we did need three people.'

On the boat, Chrissie had arranged for Tyler and Arthur to be removed from the cabin first. The stretcher-bearers moved in to take charge of them.

'There's a convoy going at eight this evening,' Malan said. 'You could go out with that. And I'll get a team to look the boat over. But a third crew man...that's looking unlikely at present. You'll have to wait and see. It's a pity 'cos there's a desperate need for boats out there.' He glanced up at *Blithe Spirit* then did a double-take. 'Good lord, man – you've got a female on board.'

'My daughter.'

'You tricked me, you bugger.'

'As good as a man. She's been engineer, nurse and deck hand. Couldn't do without her.'

'You bugger.'

Mr Sellick wanted to say a word to Tyler but the rating was out cold. A nurse had taken charge and was about to rush him away.

'You see the big tent up there,' she told Mr Sellick. 'It's being used as a triage centre. They'll be able to tell you how this man's getting on.' She repeated the information for the benefit of Joseph, who was fussing over Arthur as he lay on another stretcher.

Chrissie directed the remainder of the troops off the boat and onto the quay. They shambled forward blinking in the sunlight, thanking Mr Sellick and Chrissie before being taken off by Admiralty men, military police, and nameless officials. An RSPCA fellow had already led Lag away for a period in quarantine. An inexplicable sound of cheering came from the street above. Confusion was everywhere, but Chrissie signalled to Joseph, wanting a word before he too disappeared. She drew him to one side, away from the melee.

'What will you do?' he asked, feeling shy in her company now they weren't repairing an engine together.

'What we want to do is go back to Dunkirk, if they can find someone to replace Tyler. It may not happen – they're short of men apparently.'

'I think that's wonderful,' he said. 'It's so typical of you.'

'Jos, you're the one who stuck by your injured mate for days, and got him on the boat.' She took his arm. 'Anyway, you don't know what's typical of me.'

'That's true.' He wondered if he dared say what was in his head, then found he'd said it. 'I'd like to know, though.'

'I wouldn't mind either,' Chrissie said.

She felt like giving him a kiss, but decided it wasn't appropriate in the circumstances. Instead she shook hands, which made him smile. She still had the pencil, and scribbled her name and address on a piece of paper, handing it over without comment.

He moved reluctantly away. 'I'll see what the medics say about Arthur.'

Malan's men were already taking possession of *Blithe Spirit* but she made an excuse and went briefly back on board. She gazed at the bullet marks where Tyler had fallen, then went down into the cabin and stood amidst the dirt and detritus, which Malan's people would soon make short work of. Sounds of pandemonium on the quay drifted through the port-holes, but she was silent with her thoughts.

Back outside, Chrissie went up the harbour steps as she'd done a hundred times before and found a whole new world on the narrow pavements. Rows of stalls had been set up at the roadside and an army of women stood behind plates of rolls and cakes and biscuits, and great cans of tea. Another stand had a mound of socks, which were much in demand. There were signs saying 'WELCOME BACK BOYS' and 'WELL DONE LADS' and 'THANK YOU LADS'. A sense of tremendous excitement was in the air. Some of the men who'd been on *Blithe Spirit* were there, a few of them openly in tears, when they weren't wolfing down the food and drink. Chrissie recalled the silent reception of returning troops a week earlier and marvelled at the transformation.

She saw someone she knew slightly serving at one of the stalls; a great beefy woman with arms like hams.

'This is amazing,' Chrissie said, unable to use the woman's name because she'd forgotten it. 'What's happening here?'

'I know,' the woman said. 'The A.R.P. and the women's organisations have set things up. It's wonderful to be doing something, instead of waiting for the Nazis to invade.'

'And all this bread! You couldn't get bread for love or money.'

'No but they got hold of some flour.' She gestured down the line of stalls. 'Us women have spent the week at home baking. You can see the boys appreciate it.'

'You bet your life they do. They've not had a square meal for days. There wasn't even fresh water in Dunkirk.'

'I heard you were out there,' the woman said. 'Well done, Chrissie. Your mother's here, you know. Have you seen her?'

'*What*! *Mum*! But...she's not at all well, you know. She really shouldn't be working.'

The woman grinned. 'Are you going to be the one to tell her?'

Chrissie shook her head. 'I never have been.'

Sure enough Mrs Sellick was standing ten stalls down the line. She had an old coat round her shoulders and was tilting a damn great tea urn towards a soldier's mug. Chrissie ran down the pavement towards her.

'Mum!'

Mrs Sellick looked up. 'Hello Chrissie.'

'But...you're *here*!'

'Very observant, I'm sure.'

Chrissie ran forward to hold her mother tight. It was an unfamiliar move, but one that was tolerated on this special occasion. 'You're OK then?' Mrs Sellick said.

'I'm fine, mum. Have you seen dad?'

'I caught a glimpse of him, going the other way. Had his head up his backside as usual.'

'Oh mum!'

It was nerve-racking seeing her mother *working* out in the open, when she'd hardly been out of the house, yet Mrs Sellick looked better than she had done in weeks. Her appearance symbolised the change between the Ramsgate Chrissie had left and the one she'd come back to.

Behind Mrs Sellick a band of young boys were handing out what looked like post-cards to the returning troops.

'What's going on here?' asked Chrissie.

'Every man that comes back gets a postcard,' her mother explained. 'He puts the address of his next-of-kin on the back, and on the front he tells them he's still alive.'

'How organised.'

'It is. And you see all those buses.' A hundred yards away the road was congested with transport. 'They take men off to the station, and there are trains waiting to get them all over the country. It *is* organised. The government's got its finger out at last.'

'Mum, I'm going to find dad. He's gone to the medical tent. Someone on *Blithe Spirit* was hurt. Will you be having a rest soon?'

'Get away with you, girl.'

'Right, then I'll tell him where to find you.'

The triage tent had been set up in the middle of the fun-fair area. It struck a quaint note although the fair itself was closed. As Chrissie entered she passed her father coming out, and noted his grim expression.

'What is it, dad?'

'It's Tyler.' He pulled her just inside, away from the stream of people coming and going. 'I'm sorry girl, he's dead.'

'What! He can't be!'

'Loss of blood. They said nothing could have been done outside a hospital.'

She heard the words but her brain refused to process them. Tyler dead! She could feel the transcribed letter to his girl-friend rustling in her pocket. Dear Sandra. 'But he went so quietly,' she said.

'Yep. No kicking and screaming for him. The best men die without fuss.'

'Dad, I think he knew he was going to die.'

'People do.'

'But I didn't believe him.'

'You're doing OK, Chrissie. Don't worry about it.'

She remembered the hundreds of wounded men languishing on Dunkirk's beaches, needing medical attention and not getting it. What she and her father and Tyler had experienced on *Blithe Spirit* was a tiny element of the tragedy, which still went on.

A chair was nearby and she felt the need to sit down. 'I've seen mum,' she said. 'She's working on the stalls, handing out food and cups of tea.'

'That sounds like your mother,' said Mr Sellick.

'I didn't tell her...that we might go back.' She gave an impish smile. 'I felt that was a husband's role.'

He bowed. 'Thank you so much.'

Joseph, about to pass them on his way out of the tent, came back when he caught sight of Chrissie. Like Mr Sellick he looked grim-faced.

'I'm glad I caught you. I've had bad news about Arthur. They're not sure, but he's likely to lose his foot. He's got something they called gangrene.'

'Yes,' was Chrissie's only response.

'You don't look surprised,' Joseph said.

'I was afraid of it. I met that horrible smell once before, but I'm just an amateur nurse, so I wasn't sure. I'm sorry, Jos.'

He shook his head. 'He had such a rough time. He was sleeping in a wheel-barrow for much of the trip.' He nodded towards the interior of the tent. 'You know, there's a load of blokes in there have been put down on the hard ground. The nurses have mattresses all right but the men are too muscle-bound to tolerate them.'

'But your friend – will he live?' Chrissie enquired.

'Looks like it, thank god. I owe him so much. He took me under his wing, kept me entertained. He was so street-wise, you wouldn't believe.'

Chrissie told him about Tyler, and Joseph turned to Mr Sellick. 'I wanted to ask you about that, sir. I understand you need a third person to go back to Dunkirk. I'd like to volunteer, if you feel I can be any use to you.'

Mr Sellick's eyes lit up. 'Are you sure about that, lad? Aren't you worn out after your time on the road?'

'I'm fine, sir. I got some sleep on the boat. I've not been much use to the war effort so far, but this is my chance. Dunkirk is where it's happening. And...because of Arthur, you know.'

'And what about Chrissie?' Mr Sellick said. 'Would my daughter have anything to do with your decision?'

Joseph laughed, looking embarrassed. 'I admit she's the best-looking engineer I've met so far, sir.'

'All right, lad.' Mr Sellick reached to shake Joseph's hand. 'Welcome aboard. I'll pass the good news on to the Admiralty blokes. Now then, you come home with us, eh? You can have a meal and a few hours of sleep before we leave. I'll put you in my son's bed.'

'There's no need to do that, sir.'

'It will be an honour, lad.'

~ Seven ~

Back at 150, High Street, Chrissie introduced Joseph to the family's bath-night routine. She brought the tin hip-bath in from the back yard and poured into it boiling water from the kettle and two large saucepans. When Joseph had done with it she showed him to the bed in Tom's room, then returned to the kitchen and climbed into the bath herself. There was a strange intimacy about sharing the bathwater with a man she'd begun to be interested in. By the time *she'd* bathed, her father was back from talking to Malan. After he'd taken third shift, the bath water was virtually black.

At six in the evening Mrs Sellick woke all three of them, announcing that dinner would be ready shortly. Joseph came down dressed in an assortment of Tom's clothes that fitted him surprisingly well. Mrs Sellick served up rabbit with boiled potatoes and peas, which the mariners disposed of like people who'd not eaten for years. She addressed her husband and Chrissie with detached coolness and Joseph with solicitude.

They'd finished the last of an apple pie when Uncle Stephen arrived on a surprise visit. He sat at the table and quizzed them about conditions on the Dunkirk beaches. Without actually saying so he looked envious that the three of them had experienced what he only knew in theory.

'I'm surprised they let you out of Dover, Stephen,' Mr Sellick said. 'Isn't

Dunkirk boiling up to a finale?'

'I'll be back there shortly,' Uncle Stephen confirmed. 'We'll be at it all night. So your convoy's leaving this evening?'

'That's what they tell us.'

'Hmm. It may not be the last night of the evacuation, but it won't be far off. The Germans are gradually encroaching on the beaches. Actually, there aren't so many British troops waiting on the sands now. You might almost be better going into the harbour. And another thing. There's been so much shipping sunk in daylight, they're thinking of restricting the evacuation to the hours of darkness, though...' He sighed. 'My boss and the Admiralty don't see eye to eye about that. Communications have been a nightmare throughout the operation.'

Chrissie, Joseph and Mr Sellick were down at the harbour well before eight. Ramsgate's streets were quieter but a number of men and women had remained at their posts dealing with incoming troops. Mr Sellick met Malan at the bottom of the steps; the man never seemed to go off-duty.

'You'll be with a tug called *Angela*,' he said. 'Hope it fares better than poor old Bates on your last trip. We've cleaned up *Blithe Spirit* as best we could. They checked the temporary joint on the carburettor, as you requested, but it was such a good job they didn't meddle with it. Who did that work?'

Joseph pointed to Chrissie and she pointed to him.

'Well done anyway,' Malan said. 'Hope you're trouble-free this time, though it's asking a lot in those waters. I reckon fouled propellers are the biggest hazard. By the way, there's some VIP military johnny on the *Angela*. Can't think why at this late stage, but in any case you needn't have anything to do with him.'

Blithe Spirit was waiting for them, in a better shape than they'd left her. The cabin had been cleaned up to a condition that would have satisfied Mrs Sellick at her fussiest. Tanks for fuel and water were full. Of course, the line of bullet marks on deck by the wheel-house was still there.

They set off in the same formation as before, viz, a tug pulling four smaller boats. There was plenty of traffic en route, in the shape of ships returning laden with troops, but also small boats on their way out that the convoy overtook. They got Joseph into the wheelhouse and gave him some elementary lessons on managing a motor-boat. Steering was new to him, but he quickly got a feel for the mechanical elements.

For several hours the journey passed without incident, until the tug that was leading the convoy developed a problem. Nothing so catastrophic as the explosion on their previous tug, but it involved engine problems that the crew couldn't resolve. The vessels under tow were advised by loud hailer to finish their journey independently. Mr Sellick got *Blithe Spirit's* engines running and was about to move off when another message arrived: that they should take on board a colonel Baker and deliver him to Dunkirk harbour.

'Blimey, a colonel,' murmured Mr Sellick. 'This'll be the VIP johnnie Malan talked about. You'll have to behave yourself now, Chrissie.'

'Why us?' said Chrissie. 'Why not one of the other boats?'

'Good question. Do we take it as a compliment, or what? Either way we'd better take the bugger.'

He manoeuvred so that *Blithe Spirit* and the tug were virtually touching and the colonel crossed from one boat to the other without fuss, a feat not all military bigwigs could manage. The minute she set eyes on the newcomer Chrissie knew her father's egalitarian soul wouldn't take kindly to him. Baker was a parody of a high-ranking officer, with a ramrod back, a trimmed moustache on his upper lip, and a perfectly ironed uniform that belonged in the War Office rather than the deck of a second-hand motor boat. It got worse when the man opened his mouth to disclose an accent from Kensington or Mayfair.

'Thanks for stepping into the breach, you fellows,' Baker said, as *Blithe Spirit* continued independently for the second time in 48 hours. He introduced himself to the three crew members. Mr Sellick didn't actually say 'How can anyone who speaks like you expect to be taken seriously?' but Chrissie could see it written across his face. Baker seemed blithely unaware of the effect he had on the hoi polloi.

'If you chaps can get me into Dunkirk harbour I'd be most grateful,' he said.

'Anywhere in particular?' said Mr Sellick. 'What is it you've got to accomplish out there?'

'Afraid I'm not at liberty to reveal that, old man. Hush hush stuff, you know. Just get me into the harbour and I'll play it by ear after that.'

'We've not been in the harbour yet, so we'll both be playing by ear.'

Chrissie thought it best to get the man away from her father. She took him to the cabin and briefly described events of the previous 24 hours. He listened politely and without interruption, though his interest in nautical matters was minimal. On the other hand Joseph's experiences riveted his attention. They never did discover what Baker had been sent out to do, but he grilled Joseph for the best part of an hour on everything that had happened during his odyssey to Dunkirk. Chrissie had to interrupt when *Blithe Spirit* herself contracted an engine problem that demanded Joseph's help. She expected Baker to show irritation but he took the delay in his stride.

'Can't be helped, eh? Just get us there as soon as you can.'

Chrissie and Joseph spent an hour examining the engine without making progress. They had to work by torchlight this time, but that wasn't significant; the problem, whatever it was, happened to be more fundamental than they could handle at night in the middle of an ocean.

'It's infuriating,' Chrissie complained to Joseph as they knelt on the deck peering into *Blithe Spirit's* entrails. 'This has happened on both trips.'

'It's not surprising,' said Joseph. 'I don't suppose she's ever experienced what you've put her through in the past 48 hours.'

There was nothing for it but to make for Dunkirk on the one engine. Fortunately, the experience of the first voyage helped with navigation, despite the notorious difficulties of locating the harbour entrance. By Mr Sellick's watch it was just after midnight when the glowing cinder that was Dunkirk first showed up on the horizon. As they approached, the destroyer *Codrington* swept past them on a homeward path, fortunately at a safe distance, followed a few minutes later by another destroyer, *Sabre*. Neither ship had lights showing but the moon was strong enough to reveal the helmets of innumerable men huddled on their decks. The powerful, silent passage of these ships across the Channel's calm waters always took Chrissie's breath away.

At the harbour entrance they were met by a motorboat bearing a bouncy little chap with a searchlight and a loud-hailer.

'Commander Maund at your service,' he called, using the hailer against the intermittent sound of shells that rained down on the area.

Mr Sellick said they'd come to pick up men from the beaches or the harbour, but first they had to drop off a Colonel Baker.

'Excellent, they're expecting him,' said Maund. 'There's a welcoming party. They're in a hut behind the little lighthouse, far end of this east mole. Go past the big ships moored at this end and tie up amongst the smaller boats further in. There's a fullish tide at present so watch the draught if you're here any length of time. And mind the strong currents in the harbour. And if I were you I'd have people in the bow with torches – there are too many wrecks lurking just below the surface.'

'What about the beaches?' Mr Sellick shouted above the noise of shells and gunfire. 'Are we needed there afterwards?'

'I hesitate to advise,' said Maund. 'Some small boats have reported that beaches were empty, so they came in here to pick up troops. But the situation's changing all the time. If you decide to stay in the harbour, forget about the docks. They're burning like merry hell. The mole's the only option, though it may not look it – the thing was never designed for embarkation. Away you go and good luck to you.'

Mr Sellick posted Chrissie in the bow and Joseph on the starboard side, and ordered them to keep their eyes peeled for obstructions in the water. He cut the engine to a funereal pace and edged the vessel forward.

For weeks afterwards Chrissie had flashbacks of the remarkable scenes that now met her eyes; she was like a woman who'd experienced unusually colourful dreams or an overdose of some powerful drug. The mole loomed up stark and forbidding to port, whilst light and shade came from the dazzling phosphorescence of the sea, and shells bursting all around, and bombs from the German planes that raced overhead, all against a backdrop of burning and exploding buildings in the town. She dismissed thoughts of personal safety and in spite of herself felt the same rising tide of excitement as before.

As they went into harbour she was relieved they didn't need to berth near the entrance. How the big ships had managed to do so safely she could only surmise. She saw the minesweeper *Duchess of Fife* roped to the mole, followed by a stretch where a burnt-out troop ship had gone to the bottom, then the destroyer *Icarus*, a pleasure steamer called *Royal Daffodil* and another destroyer. On *Icarus's* foc'sle was a bagpiper in full regalia, sending his mournful wail across the waters.

The mole wasn't the sort of construction she'd expected, confirming Maund's information that it was 'not designed for embarkation'. It had also been badly damaged by German bombing, and no doubt by the recent and unfamiliar use. She remembered something Tyler had said – she thought about Tyler all the time – to the effect that destroyers, built for speed, had exceptionally thin plating along their sides, and had to be manoeuvred skilfully alongside to avoid damage; whereas passenger vessels, designed for use with a variety of quays and piers, were fitted with thick rubbing strakes from bow to stern.

Ever observant, Chrissie noted that on several ships the decks – even with a highish tide – came four or five feet below the mole, so troops had to negotiate unfamiliar ladders or poles to embark. She watched as one man after another threw his (presumably loaded) rifle down to the deck before descending, and wondered whether this led to some unfortunate accidents.

Something that would have upset a less hard-boiled woman than Chrissie was the business of the dogs. To a ridiculous extent the canines of the Dunkirk hinterland had left their homes – no doubt abandoned by their owners – and attached themselves to dog-loving British Tommies. Any number of them were frisking about on the mole; when within range of the bagpiper they emitted high-pitched howls that combined with the caterwauling of the pipes to blood-curdling effect. Sadly, the dog exodus had an unhappy ending, because the military police weren't allowing them onto ships; they shot the creatures and threw their bodies into the sea, roundly booed by the men. Their carcasses floated on the water's surface.

Chrissie didn't actually see any German projectiles strike the mole, but a cursory glance revealed the damage that shelling had done, and she saw two working parties of sappers making repairs. Negotiating the walkway looked hazardous in the extreme; even as she watched, a soldier tripped and disappeared from view, and she heard the splash as his body hit the water.

Towards the farther end of the mole colonel Baker approached Chrissie as she stood in the bow. She was concentrating so hard on her look-out duties she'd forgotten he was there. Since he'd not got onto name terms and Chrissie didn't have a rank, he settled on 'Miss'.

'Did you get anywhere with that busted engine, miss?'

'We couldn't do it,' she answered.

'I see. So what happens on your return journey?'

'We try and get back on the one engine, though it means carrying fewer troops. Or just possibly we might get a tow.'

'Suppose I get a couple of royal engineers to look at it. Those chaps can fix most things, what!'

She stared at him. She wanted to tell him nobody used the expression 'What!' in that way outside a comedy show. Instead she said 'But can you do that? I mean, would they bother to help a small boat like ours?'

'They will if I ask them.'

As they talked, her father was guiding *Blithe Spirit* towards a space on the mole. Between them and the lighthouse a plethora of small boats bobbed on the water – skoots, drifters, motor yachts, whalers. The occasional shell whined overhead and plunged into the deep.

'Well colonel,' she said, unconvinced that his plan was remotely a goer, 'Of course, if it's at all possible that would be good. How would it work exactly?'

'I'll have to locate the chaps I'm thinking of,' he said. 'May take a bit of time. How about one of your crew comes with me into town and waits somewhere under cover – and I'll bring them to you, eh?'

By now Mr Sellick had the boat beside the mole. French troops were milling about on the walkway, none of them keen to grab a line, so Chrissie used their ladder to get herself on top and tied up to a Samson post. They conferred about Baker's suggestion and Mr Sellick jumped at the idea; he never felt happy unless both engines were operational. They had a brief but tetchy exchange about whether she should be the one to accompany the colonel. Chrissie argued that she'd be safer (albeit not safe) somewhere on land rather than being a sitting duck in the harbour, and Mr Sellick reluctantly concurred. In fact she couldn't wait to see what conditions were like in the town. Her father had often said curiosity would be the death of her, and she was about to put it to the test.

'We'll wait here for an hour,' Mr Sellick told the colonel. 'Longer than that and I'll assume it's no go. In which case you come back, Chrissie, and we'd take a limited number of troops on board and get the hell out of here.'

So Chrissie found herself negotiating the mole in the company of an army officer. His seniority encouraged British soldiers to make way for them, French troops less so. Progress along the top was far from straightforward. She marvelled that the uncertain structure had served to embark men in their tens of thousands. They were essentially moving down a plank-way just wide enough to accommodate three men standing abreast. The sides were protected by wooden railings, though there were frequent gaps in these and for that matter in the planking under foot. A moment's inattention could be disastrous. Once Chrissie stumbled and might have gone over the edge had Baker not seized her arm. He moved quickly, sure-footed as a mountain goat, and she had to exert herself to keep up with him.

At the lighthouse an army captain and an orderly stepped smartly forward and Baker returned their salutes. He explained Chrissie's presence and enquired about a place that could serve as a rendez-vous later on. All four of them then pressed on into the town itself. Here Chrissie's curiosity was satisfied, and in spades. She'd never conceived of anything like it. Progress through the town was only possible on foot. The streets were littered with debris where house-fronts had collapsed outwards. A row of warehouses, burning fiercely, emitted a tremendous heat, and flames spat up through gaps in the pavements. Their footsteps crunched from walking on a thousand shards of glass. Dead bodies lay untended and she recognised the odour of blood amongst the fumes of cordite and burning oil. Like most people in the streets they coughed and spluttered whilst moving along. The light was absurdly bright for a town that was without power in the middle of the night.

As they rounded a corner Baker grabbed Chrissie and yanked her into his arms. Before she could protest a terrified horse charged past, narrowly missing them both. She got a glimpse of its flaring nostrils and felt the animal's hide scrape against her. Further down the street an ammunition truck had caught fire and was going off in all directions. She thought of her father and Jos moored under the mole and hoped they were safe, but had no wish to be anywhere but where she was. She revelled in the town's crazy atmosphere.

'This could be the place for you,' said Baker. 'Hardly ideal, but my chaps reckon it's the best we're going to find.'

They'd stopped outside a building that had been some kind of drinking establishment. The name was displayed over the entrance, but as some letters were missing and others dangled uselessly, the title remained a mystery.

'It's an *estaminet*,' Baker explained, a word that meant nothing to her. 'Hang around here and I'll get back soon as I can. You should be safe enough.'

'If anywhere is safe,' she said.

'And if the French don't get you. Cheerie-bye for now.'

Within seconds Baker and the other two had gone, leaving Chrissie standing on what passed for a pavement outside the anonymous *estaminet*. She stared open-mouthed at the stuff going on around her. Somehow or other the owners had rigged up a power source so that the café blazed with light, making it an ideal target for German shells. The place was also distinguished by its crush of troops, British and French, that thronged inside and spilled out into the street, many of them clutching wine glasses. It struck her they were behaving like Ramsgate citizens outside the Vale Road Tavern, on a summer's Saturday evening shortly before closing time.

'What is this place?' she enquired of a tubby British corporal.

'This here? Dontcha know the Cafe de Fleurs?' He gestured extravagantly, slopping wine from his glass.

'Fleurs. That's "flowers", isn't it?'

'Search me, lady.'

Her shifts at the Vale Road Tavern had given Chrissie a good grasp of male inebriation and she judged this man to be well over the limit. Had she been working the bar in Ramsgate she'd have refused to serve him. But there was clearly nobody 'at the bar' in this establishment; alcohol was freely available from an as yet undisclosed source. It accounted for the buoyant mood amongst the assembled company, merry but not yet maudlin. These troops might almost have forgotten that a war was raging outside; that at any moment a German shell could blow the lot of them sky-high. Perhaps that was the point, she thought.

Unusually, Chrissie was not the only female present. At least three other women were about, all French, all indulging as if there were no tomorrow. And local men too, one of them in the traditional French beret.

'Don't tell me people are still living here?' she asked the tubby corporal.

'That's right, lady. You wouldn't want to miss a party like this, would you?'

'There's a lot of 'em what are down in the cellars,' tubby's mate told her. 'Waiting for the Boche to arrive. They'll be OK, long as they're not in uniform.'

A French soldier detached himself from the crowd and bowed towards Chrissie, clicking his heels. She knew he was some sort of officer from the gubbins on his shoulders, not to mention the man's overweening self-confidence. He addressed her with the familiar French flourish, as if every word he spoke was of earth-shaking importance. Chrissie was amused but found she liked it.

She'd never had formal tuition in the language, yet discovered from dealing with French sailors in Ramsgate that she was quick to pick up its essentials. Even so, she'd not understood a word the officer had said.

'*Pardonne,*' she told him. '*Je suis Anglais.*'

'*Tant pis,*' he responded. 'Mademoiselle ees very sharming.'

'Drives me up the wall the way they speak English,' said the tubby corporal in an aside to his mate.

'Only fing worse is the way they speak French,' said the mate.

'Mademoiselle she permit?' The officer indicated his own wine glass. '*Un verre de vin?*'

'Oh, *tres charmant,*' said tubby.

'*Plume de ma tante*,' said the mate, apparently under the impression they were a double act.

Though she'd worked in a pub Chrissie had never tasted wine, and didn't want it now. Besides, she needed to keep a clear head for the hours to come. But she wanted to retain the Frenchman's attention, because he was the most attractive man she'd ever set eyes on.

'*Merci*,' she told him, 'But only *un peu*.' She mimed with thumb and forefinger. '*Un peu, vraiment*.'

'*Oui, oui, oui*.' Like all the French nation he was devoted to their absurd word for 'Yes'. '*Attendez un moment*.'

He about-turned and plunged into the fray, returning with another glass of red wine in hand.

The Brit double-act evaporated in the face of competition and Chrissie's new friend urged her to take a sip.

'Try eet, mademoiselle.'

She sipped and restrained herself from pulling a face. It tasted nothing like any alcohol she'd tried before, or wanted to try again.

'You do not like?'

'*Je ne sais pas,*' she said. She thought about removing his hand from her waist but it felt good there.

Then 'You are 'ungry, non?'

'Why angry? Of course not. *Je suis satisfait*.'

'Non, non, mademoiselle. 'Ungry. Com faim.' He made an eating motion.

'Oh, *hungry*! Well...I like to eat, yes, but...surely you don't have food in here?'

'We 'ave *ragout*,' he said. 'You like?'

Chrissie thought she'd misunderstood, then noticed that several French soldiers in the place were eating. And was she imagining things, or could that be the aroma of cooked mutton?

'*Ragout?*,' she repeated. '*C'est possible*?'

'*Naturellement*.' He shrugged in the Gallic way. '*Un moment*.'

Off he went again, leaving Chrissie wondering what she'd let herself in for. In Ramsgate, if a man took a girl to the pictures two or three times, he'd expect to kiss her afterwards. What was the going rate for a dish of ragout in the dying hours of free France? She considered making a bolt for it, but the urge to stay was stronger.

He was back in no time with two plates of food, and took her to a small table against the wall. Two French soldiers readily made way for their officer, though he was was polite about it, scattering some 'pardons' around. Perhaps it was a consequence of time and place but the food tasted wonderful. Naturellement – this was France! The officer ate with delicate manners, something she always appreciated. The table was so small their heads almost touched as they consumed the meal. Beneath it, the man had one of Chrissie's legs clasped between his, and a knee in her crotch. Her appetite waned as desire welled up with a carnal fierceness she'd not known before.

Chrissie was not experienced with men – least of all French men – but something told her an invitation would follow the meal. She fretted about engaging in such light-hearted behaviour (actually, not *that* light-hearted) when men were dying all around. She wondered what British soldiers would think of her fraternising with the enemy, then remembered that the French were on the same side.

Sure enough the officer rose to his feet and invited her to go to the back of the building. She didn't bother to feign reluctance. They went through a side door, away from the blazing light and into an unlit corridor. She found herself in a kind of pantry, dimly illuminated by flames from a burning building nearby. There were shelves with cleaning materials, a scrubbing brush and a plastic bucket, and he kissed very nicely. A faint scent of cologne came from his face. She remembered colonel Baker saying 'If the French don't get you'. Part of her regretted that the trousers she was wearing would preserve her virginity, though his hand found a route into them, touching in a way that made Chrissie unsteady on her feet. She plunged a hand into *his* trousers and was amazed by what it found. Nothing daunted she drew the thing out and familiarised herself with its contours, until it went berserk in her fingers.

Then he was nice to her and tried to scrub the stain from the knee of her trousers. By now she'd come to her senses, remembering that Baker might return to collect her, and got away as fast as she decently could. She stood out on the blistered pavement watching shells drop in the distance, thinking how little she knew and how much she wanted to know, realising she hadn't asked his name. British soldiers offered her drinks and she gave them the cold shoulder, except to check on the time. Time had little meaning in Dunkirk that night but Mr Sellick's one-hour deadline buzzed in her head. Baker didn't reappear, and she knew how silly she'd been to think a senior officer would honour his promise to a nobody girl from Ramsgate. She walked a few yards down the road and realised she'd forgotten the route back to the quayside.

'Jolly good – glad to meet up again,' said a voice in her ear. The colonel was back, together with two young men whom he introduced as royal engineers. 'Sorry about the hold-up,' he went on. 'Punctuality goes to pot in war, what!'

She almost threw her arms round his neck, and smiled at the thought of his reaction – 'Dashed impudence, what!'.

'My regards to your father,' he said. 'These young fellows'll get you back to the boat all right. May even mend that blasted engine, eh?' And off he went on his mystery mission. And off Chrissie went with a revised opinion of crusty military officers.

*** *** ***

After his brief encounter with Joseph and Arthur under the glade of trees, Captain Hardy became separated from General Gort's group of senior officers. Another captain – a man Hardy knew well – had been nursing a stomach ache for some time, and not wanting to make a fuss had concealed it from his colleagues. This was a mistake because he was suffering from a rumbling appendix, which only became obvious when that futile organ burst inside him. He needed proper medical treatment but Gort's mission couldn't be delayed, so Hardy volunteered to stay with his stricken colleague at a provincial hospital. Whether prompt treatment would have made a difference no-one was ever to know. The man died the following day and Hardy stayed on to attend his burial. He stood in the small cemetery as two grave-diggers lowered the coffin, his only other company a Catholic priest. The colleague's identity tag was in his pocket.

Hardy had told Joseph and Arthur to 'make for Dunkirk', and he now had to follow his own advice, albeit without the motorbike. He quickly found that going it alone was different from travelling in one of Gort's staff cars. He'd filled a rucksack with a change of clothing, some provisions and a decent sized bottle of water, and set off on foot. Within the first two hours this load got lighter because of encounters on the way, the first comical, the second utterly tragic. Because the hospital had been off the beaten track he started on minor roads, with few troops of any kind for company. The first soldier he met could only be identified as British by his helmet. This apparition was walking on the grass verge of the road, barefoot and in his underpants, still carrying his rifle. The man explained how this came about. He and three other privates had waded through a canal after finding a bridge blown, each of them carrying different equipment on their heads, but the man carrying all the clothes had become separated from the others. Hardy took pity on him and surrendered his spare trousers and socks, sorry that he couldn't provide boots as well.

He found the second incident hard to shift from his mind. It was unusual to see German tanks around Dunkirk because the plethora of canals and rivers rendered the terrain unsuitable. However for once he saw the gruesome aftermath of a tank attack, as half a dozen men lay by the roadside with appalling wounds. He was of no help medically but couldn't resist their pathetic cries for water. By the time he walked away his own water bottle was empty. A kilometre further on he nearly met one of the tanks, recognising the familiar grinding sound coming up fast from the rear. The road was lined on both sides with head-high hedges. Hardy just about scrambled over one, landing – covered in scratches – on its far side where he was balefully regarded by a cow. He sat in the field for a while waiting till the coast was clear, talking to the animal. It occurred to him that he was beginning to relish the experience of being alone, caring only for his own skin and free of any responsibility for others. It was a long time since that had been the case.

Blessed with a good sense of direction, Hardy had no trouble picking which roads to use. If not certain he'd check with a resident, using his half-decent French. The local people were never hostile but their preoccupations matched his own. He saw many sad things on the road, the worst of them a primary school which for some unfathomable reason had been bombed, so that rows of meagre shrouds were laid out in the playground.

As Hardy closed on Dunkirk the roads grew broader and more British troops moved along them, mostly on foot. There was no concealing his captain rank, unusual enough amongst foot-sloggers to excite comment. He missed the congenial company of his own peer group but didn't try to ingratiate himself with other ranks. Moving amongst the troops in this way he began to gauge their morale. Spirits were noticeably higher amongst units that had been in action. What most concerned him was the chaotic nature of the retreat, which could only be ascribed to the officer corps, of which he was a part.

Once in a while a staff car would stop, allowing him to exchange a few words with its passengers. In this way Hardy gathered insights into the deployment of the British Expeditionary Force across a broad front. The vehicles were invariably crammed with officers, so there was no question of a lift. He was glad about this; he could feel his body strengthening from the unfamiliar exercise, and relished the sensation.

Hardy nearly came unstuck when he took a chance and detoured across a couple of fields. Arriving at the bridge he'd been aiming for, he found it had been blown. But bridges impassable to wheels remained vulnerable to men on foot; he was able to slide down one side of the ruins and climb up the other, barely getting his feet wet in the middle.

On the last stretch of road he was weary, no doubt about it. Now he'd have appreciated a lift, but the flood of troops on foot meant that vehicles progressed no faster than people. He longed for something to drink. He'd refilled his water bottle just once since helping out the tank casualties, and was experiencing the anguish of extreme thirst. Trudging past hundreds of vehicles abandoned at the roadside the captain thought of searching for water in them. He chose a lorry with dozens of unopened crates in the back and hoisted himself over the tailgate to investigate. The first crate was tough to break down but yielded to a makeshift tool. Inside were boxes of marshmallows, which were difficult to swallow with a parched mouth. Effing and blinding, he forced a second crate in a different part of the lorry, envisaging bottles of spring water or (his personal pipe dream) ginger beer. The crate opened to reveal...pairs of socks. He left the whole lot where they were and got back on the road.

It was gone midnight when Hardy passed through the shell-shocked streets of Dunkirk, with their furtive figures flitting round the edges of buildings, and thrust past the dunes onto the flat terrain of the Dunkirk beaches. After the congested roads, the open expanse held an immediate appeal. He tasted the salt on his lips and heard the wet sand squelch under his boots. Not far away a shadowy group of soldiers sat round a fire, but few others were in sight. A mile or so away a red glow signified the harbour, from which the distant sound of gunfire carried along the shore.

He took some paces in that direction but knew instantly that it was beyond him. Down he went, literally on his knees, then his back. Seaweed felt flabby against his hand. Despite the raging thirst he knew sleep would come. Black clouds drifted across the sky as his eyes closed. Waves broke on the shore.

When the captain opened his eyes again dawn was starting. A shaft of light crept along the horizon, though the sands remained dark and sullen. He checked his watch: 4.45am. He'd slept for a mere four hours yet felt remarkably refreshed. He sat up to scan the beach in both directions. The harbour glow was the only sign of life. The men round the bonfire had made themselves scarce and nobody else was within sight. It occurred to Hardy that he'd been left for dead; that the prone figure in the greatcoat had been seen as one more corpse amongst the many strewn along the coast.

He climbed to his feet brushing sand from his clothes. There was a residual stiffness but none of the exhaustion from a few hours earlier. It was decision time. Far out at sea a couple of ships sat on the horizon, but nothing was remotely close. With no more ado he stepped out for the harbour. If he had doubts they related to thirst, which was undermining his strength. It had been 20 hours since water passed his lips. He'd not taken a piss for the same length of time.

Half way to the harbour Hardy found his life-saver, though he almost walked straight past it. By this stage of the Dunkirk story the sands and the adjacent shallows were littered with abandoned boats of all kinds. Something – perhaps its respectable condition – caused him to look twice at the large sailing barge standing upright six feet from the water's edge. It was a substantial vessel, perhaps 80 feet in length, with the name *Doris* clearly emblazoned on its hull. Hardy had a maiden aunt called Doris, and the boat's chunky, broad-beamed appearance brought her to mind, no less than the dirty-red colour of the sail, which matched a blouse he'd once seen on his aunt's washing line. With no great expectations – after his dud discovery of the marshmallows – he hopped over the rail to investigate. In the hold he found dozens of full water casks and a pile of army rations, all – as far as he could see – untouched. He gave silent thanks to the skipper who'd beached *Doris* at this spot, then sat in the bow and consumed a pint of water, biscuits with pilchard paste, fruit cake, then more water. It was the best meal of his life.

After he'd filled his water bottle and put food in the rucksack, something made Hardy check his watch again. Gort's officers were provided with good timepieces that gave the date as well as the hour, and he noted from the former that 24 hours of his life had gone missing. It struck him that he'd not slept for four hours after all but for 28 hours, which was why he felt so refreshed. As he jumped onto the sand to started walking again the captain found himself whistling.

Arriving at the harbour, Hardy saw a tremendous throng of troops milling around the start of the mole, effectively blocking access to it. He reckoned three-quarters of these, at the very least, were French. He'd heard that French units tended to stick together at embarkation, and now saw a whole regiment of them, loaded with equipment – even bikes – but precious little in the way of arms. His officer eyes recoiled from some of the ancient gear. A bunch of reservists were in 1914 uniforms.

At the beginning of the pier a British officer in a slit trench was trying to impose order by allocating numbers for groups of men around him, then calling the numbers when ships became available. Even so there was chaos on the walkway as individuals complicated these attempts at an orderly embarkation.

As a lone, unattached officer, Hardy was in an unusual position. He knew General Gort's band of senior staff would have embarked on one of the big ships, and by now be back in Dover. Hardy had no men to command and didn't fit naturally into the groups queueing for embarkation. He was determined not to pull rank on anyone, having a fastidious sense of reserve about 'jumping the queue'. He knew that the Germans were pressing hard, and time was running out. A sense of fatalism was entering his soul: that he'd be stuck in this place as the Germans overran the beaches; that years of his prime would be passed in a prisoner-of-war camp.

He finally got himself onto the mole – from curiosity more than anything else – and marvelled at the precarious nature of the walkway. He joined a file of men pressing for access to a minesweeper, but was turned away when the vessel filled up. The sound of the BBC's '*ITMA*' blasting from the ship's radio sent a pang of homesickness through him, though he'd never liked the programme. He perked up as the skipper of a motorboat sang out 'Room for two more', but the man next to him pleaded for his friend to go instead, and Hardy motioned them both on board.

He was about to leave the mole and return to the beaches when a voice came up from the sea below: 'Captain Hardy. Captain Hardy. Down here, sir.'

***   ***   ***

The two young engineers identified by colonel Baker were down-to-earth characters, and guided Chrissie rapidly through the desolate streets towards the harbour. They called her 'Miss' and took her arm whenever the going was difficult. One of them carried a heavy bag of equipment that boded well.

Blithe Spirit was exactly where she'd left her, albeit tucked in as close as possible to the pier for protection. Joseph received Chrissie with undisguised relief, her father more matter-of-factly. 'I'd almost given you up,' he said.

She introduced the sappers and Joseph led both to the troublesome engine. After 15 minutes one of them popped up to announce it was a transmission problem.

'Can you fix it?' asked Mr Sellick.

'I think so, sir, but it'll take best part of an hour.'

'Do your best then.'

There was nothing for it but to wait; wait amidst the sound and light show that was the Dunkirk harbour.

'So, dad,' Chrissie teased her father, 'The nice colonel man turned up trumps after all'.

Mr Sellick grunted. 'It's a miracle. Those buggers usually need someone else to wipe their arses for them.'

Chrissie had been in good spirits walking back to the harbour, but seeing Joseph again was like a dose of cold water down the back of her neck. She'd no regrets about her encounter with the French officer – Chrissie didn't do regrets – but was surprised to find herself feeling awkward in Joseph's company. Not that he noticed anything amiss. He made her a cup of coffee and asked if she'd like anything to eat.

'Don't fuss Jos,' she told him.

'But you're OK?' he pressed.

'Of course I'm OK.'

'That's all that matters then.'

The engineers' time estimate was remarkably accurate, and after 'the best part of an hour' one of them reappeared and asked Mr Sellick to activate the engine. Chrissie's father wasn't a big one for smiling, but his expression changed as the familiar throbbing noise broke out again.

'I'm beholden to you,' he told the young men. He made them write down the name and unit of their commanding officer. The engineers were anxious to get away but Chrissie got them to show her what they'd done, and Joseph tagged along.

After that Chrissie, her father and Joseph got together in the wheelhouse.

'What now?' she said.

Mr Sellick peered dubiously at the sky, where a suggestion of daylight penetrated the usual fumes of cordite and burning oil. He started to speak, then waited while a German fighter plane roared overhead strafing the mole, amidst the cries of men on the walkway.

'It's getting light,' he resumed, 'And we all know what that means. All things considered I think we'd do best to cut and run. At least with both engines running we can take a full load back with us. I know...' He held up a hand to forestall his daughter's comment. 'It's not how we imagined this second run, but that's war for you. You were going to say, Chrissie?'

'I was going to agree with you, father.'

'Blimey.'

'And to say that at least we performed the valuable service of delivering colonel Baker.

Mr Sellick ignored her. 'Joseph? Any thoughts?'

'Whatever you reckon, sir. No-one could have anticipated the engine problems.'

'All right then.' Mr Sellick look at the mole looming above them. 'Let's take on board 25 men good and true, then get the hell out of here. Only thing is...'

Chrissie grinned. 'I know. The mole's swarming with Froggies. Dammit, they're *all* Froggies.'

There were a few moments of contemplative silence.

'They were kind to Arthur and me,' said Joseph, thinking of the first aid post that dressed Arthur's wound, and the Sisters of Mercy at Zuydcoote hospital.

'They're not so bad,' said Chrissie, thinking of the French officer in the Café de Fleurs.'

'Then if we're all agreed...' Mr Sellick set up the eight-foot ladder that Malan had provided for this trip, and called to the troops above. Sure enough, the boots and backsides that clambered down the ladder were French boots and backsides. As seemed to happen with the French, there was a shortage of arms and a surfeit of equipment. Mr Sellick tolerated the attaché cases, clucking his tongue, but baulked at the man who manhandled a bike down the ladder; he dashed forward to seize the offending vehicle and hurl it into the drink.

'*Non, non, non*,' he cried out, for the benefit of the others, '*Pas des bicyclettes*'.

Chrissie and Joseph directed the first batch of 15 into the cabin, then another ten onto the deck above it. It was easier said than done. There was a lot of fuss and gesticulation, and fervent protestations in a French that they fortunately didn't understand, before the boarders twigged that *Blithe Spirit's* owners were determined to have their own way. The noise levels exceeded anything the boat had seen before.

'I didn't reckon on this,' murmured Mr Sellick. 'Oh well, grin and bear it.'

Chrissie took the wheel while her father and Joseph stood – to port and starboard respectively – scanning the inky deep for any sign of a sunken vessel that might terminate the whole enterprise. Chrissie slowed to allow the passenger steamer, *Manxman*, to pull away from the mole before them, and this was the moment when Joseph spotted Hardy on the walkway and called out to him.

'You know this man?' said Mr Sellick.

'Yes sir.' Joseph explained how they met. 'Could we take him?'

'Another bloody officer!' Mr Sellick sighed. 'All right then – at least he's English. Take her in, Chrissie, and mind how you go.'

Up went the ladder again, and Hardy descended nimbly, rucksack on his back. He helped Joseph get the ladder down, then shook his hand.

'It's Edwards, isn't it?'

'That's right, sir,' said Joseph, astonished that Hardy had remembered the name.

Joseph introduced him to the other two.

'Thanks for taking me, sir,' Hardy told Mr Sellick. 'Where are you making for?'

'Ramsgate, if we're lucky. Do you speak French?'

'Well...'

'Good.' He gestured towards the Gallic cacophony bursting from the cabin. 'Perhaps you can help us keep this lot in order.'

~ Eight ~

The main dangers to life and limb within the harbour came from ships colliding with other ships or striking half-submerged vessels, or fighter planes machine-gunning the walkway. German shelling from the Gravelines area had been persistent throughout the evacuation, but because of poor visibility caused by the burning oil tanks had never achieved much accuracy. So *Blithe Spirit* was unlucky to be leaving harbour just when a shell struck the mole.

The noise of the impact brought the most frightening moment of Chrissie's war. From the corner of an eye she saw French soldiers blown clean off the walkway and into the water. A moment later came the secondary effects. The boat was horribly thrown about in the water and Chrissie was pitched backwards onto the deck. Lumps of shell and concrete struck the infrastructure, bringing cries of pain came from the Frenchmen on deck. Chrissie registered all of it, but only had eyes for one detail. Mr Sellick, standing outside to monitor their forward passage, staggered and would have gone overboard had Hardy not leapt to seize his falling figure and drag him into the wheelhouse. Chrissie was gripped by panic, but she made herself look at him, sprawled half-sitting against the bulwark. He was conscious and white-faced, with a dark stain on his clothing near one armpit.

'Dad, dad.' She could hear the screech of panic in her voice.

'Keep your eyes on the water,' he said, in a manner that sounded nothing like him. 'Keep Joseph watching the surface for obstructions. Get us out of the harbour before you do anything else.'

'But I want to check on you,' she said.

'I'm OK, Chrissie. They'll not get rid of me that easily. When you're out of the harbour, set the course I'll give you and put Joseph at the wheel.' She was impressed by how clearly he could think after the injury. 'Then check the boat, especially the hull. That sort of shock can open the seams. Is she steering OK?'

'I think so. My hands are shaking so much...'

'Don't worry about that. When you've checked the boat then check the men up on deck. There'll be injuries.'

'Yes, yes, all right.' She felt a measure of control returning, though her hands didn't belong to her. The entrance to the harbour was looming up fast. 'Are we in the clear, Jos?' she cried.

'Straight ahead. Don't veer to port,' he warned.

'There were panicky cries from above and Mr Sellick motioned to Hardy. 'I wonder, captain, would you mind having a look round on deck. A voice of authority might be just what they need.'

'Of course.'

'And thanks for what you did just now. I was all but in the drink.'

'It's nothing, sir.' Their new recruit gave a sort of smile. 'Though...I was afraid you were going to say "Kiss me, Hardy".'

They heard Hardy addressing the men above. Even in a foreign language he managed to sound authoritative. The clamour of French voices quietened significantly.

'It's not good up there,' he said on rejoining them. 'There's one dead and another all but, if I'm any judge. Plus three more nasty injuries. Shells are a horrible weapon. They're what our chaps fear most – those secondary effects. Does anyone on board have medical training?'

'I've been on a first aid course,' said Chrissie.

'So!' Hardy raised his eyebrows. 'Chief cook and bottle-washer, eh?'

'I think it's a case of "A little knowledge is a dangerous thing," but I'll do my best.' She peered at the sky. 'There's a lot of aircraft noise up there. Do we need to worry?'

'Believe it or not, they're all British,' said Hardy. 'No kidding. The RAF are doing us proud today.'

'Long may it last.'

She set a course, on her father's instruction, and put Joseph at the wheel. In practice the number of British vessels going home by the same route made navigation fairly straightforward. Little was coming the other way, towards Dunkirk.

Chrissie began a tour of inspection, concentrating on the starboard side, which had been facing the mole when the shell hit. Hardy offered to accompany her. It could have been worse but it could also have been better. Several of *Blithe Spirit's* ribs were smashed, and one of the fresh water tanks was split asunder. The serious problem was in the hull, as her father had surmised. Chrissie was no expert but she reckoned some of the seams had sprung.

'Is there a way of dealing with that?' asked Hardy.

'I'll see what dad thinks. The sea's calm, thank heavens, or else...' She shuddered. 'I don't want to think about that. We've got a manual pump but it's a swine to operate. If I'm right about the seams we'll eventually flood below the motor bed. There may come a point when we'll be bailing with saucepans and all that malarkey. Don't know how much help these French blokes'll be.'

'You leave that to me,' said Hardy. 'Show me what needs doing and I'll get after 'em.'

'Thank you,' she said with feeling. 'You're a very big help.'

She reported back to her father, reluctant to bother him but knowing it had to be done. 'We won't know how bad it is till we get going,' he said. 'We could go back to the harbour if you like.'

'No,' said Chrissie, very quickly.

'OK, so we keep going and monitor the situation regularly. Get our usual speed down by a third, to reduce the up-and-down movement.'

Chrissie altered their speed, then introduced Hardy to the hand pump drill, then went on deck with the first aid box. She wasn't looking forward to the task, partly from an awareness of her own inadequacy. They'd told her on the Red Cross course that a confident manner was the next best thing to technical knowledge, so she tried to present a front. The deck was a war zone, with lots of blood on the woodwork. Two men had died and others needed urgent attention. The soldiers themselves showed her the most serious case. She cut away the man's shirt to find a big hole in his chest. Malan's first aid box had been well thought out, and she was able to pack the wound with vaseline, gauze and tulle as the Red Cross had told them. The man's companions noticeably perked up. Encouraged, she gestured for them to keep the casualty warm, and moved on to staunch another blood injury with padding and bandages. A shattered femur temporarily defeated her, until she thought of taping it to the butt of a rifle. She distributed pain-killers and told the company there would be '*un docteur apres quatre heures*, in Ramsgate. They gave her a little round of applause and she left the deck feeling a fraud.

Only then could Chrissie allow herself to attend her father. She cleaned her hands with surgical spirit and cut away Mr Sellick's shirt at the shoulder.

'What are you doing?' he said.

'Relax, dad. I know you like your clothes to be "just right", but I need to check your wound.'

'Have you looked at the Froggies on deck?'

'Yes dad. Now it's your turn.'

She saw with a little jump of hope that the shirt at his shoulder was torn both front and back and that the skin too was broken on both sides. Was it too much to hope that a fragment of shell had gone in and straight out again? She applied antiseptic and a dressing and gave him a pat on the chest.

'That's enough fussing,' he said. 'Go and talk to Joseph.'

'And you have a nap, why don't you.'

Joseph had questions about handling the boat. They stood at the wheel for a long time watching *Blithe Spirit's* bow plunge through the somnolent sea. The deck trembled beneath their feet. She liked the grey atmosphere, the sense of a sky about to deliver rain, though it never did. The boat wallowed and she knew they were shipping water, though Joseph was unaware of it.

She looked round and saw that her father was dozing. Without him, the sense of responsibility weighed upon her. Most days of Chrissie's life it was her and a car engine in the Ramsgate garage, and if she got it wrong the boss was there to put her right. Out here, no. Men were dying a few feet above her head. The boat might founder and sink. She could steer badly and land them on the Goodwins. 'Chief cook and bottle-washer,' Hardy had called her. She liked that and she didn't. Either way, nothing would be the same again. In three days, a dozen doors had opened. Jos stood beside her secure in his own skin, and she was unexpectedly insecure in hers.

'So much depending on you,' he said, echoing her thoughts.

'On all of us.'

'You've been amazing.'

'Don't, Jos. I don't want compliments.'

'Why do you say that?'

She turned to face him. 'Are you good at telling lies?' she asked.

'That's a strange thing to ask.'

'*Are* you?'

He looked down at the deck, shaking his head. 'My family tell me I'm rubbish. If I try to lie, they know immediately.'

'That's a good thing, surely?'

'I suppose. How about you?'

She held his gaze so intently he imagined her eyes could bore right through him. 'If anything's going to start, I want it to be clear and above board. When I went on shore back there, something happened. There was a café with loads of people, including a French officer. I went round the back with him. I'm still a virgin, but it was an experience like I've never had before.'

'There's no need...' Joseph began.

'No, let me finish. I'd had a glass of wine but I wasn't drunk or anything like that. I'm not sorry it happened. I enjoyed it. It wasn't till I got back to the boat and saw you that I felt awkward.'

He put a hand on her shoulder to stop the flow. 'Can I speak now?'

'You have my permission.'

'Yes ma'am.' He saluted. 'You remember Arthur?'

'Of course I do.'

'One of his sayings was "Things happen in wartime".' I have a story too if you'd like to hear it.'

'That's for you to decide.'

'We were spending the night in a barn belonging to this farm. When I was on my own the farmer's young wife came in. I'd been giving Arthur this big story about Methodists saving bed for marriage, but she and I...we did it...or she did it...anyway, it happened. Arthur never let me forget it.'

'I can see you tell better stories than me,' she said. 'And did you enjoy it?'

Joseph blushed very red. 'I can't say...yes, yes, it was amazing.'

Now she laughed. 'I see what your family means about your not being able to lie.'

'I know.'

Without warning she stepped between Joseph and the wheel and kissed him, and went on kissing him. For a time – how long he didn't know – he was conscious only of her body against him and her mouth unreservedly against his mouth.

'*Oi*!' Mr Sellick had woken, his mariner's instincts reacting to the lurch of the boat. 'Watch your steering.'

Joseph seized the wheel, embarrassed, and Chrissie's father relapsed into sleep.

'You're so easily blown off course,' Chrissie murmured. 'Look Jos, it's not easy to stay in touch during wartime but that was something for you to be going on with. Now you know where I stand. And another thing. It doesn't bother me your being a Methodist, but I'm my father's heathen daughter and I always will be, OK?'

'Of course it's OK.'

She left him and went up on deck to check the casualties. The wounded men were asleep, which she took as a good sign. Then to the cabin, where Hardy had one of the French soldiers on the hand pump.

He gave her a wry look.

'This pump's a bugger. The men are willing – most of them, anyway – but they can only manage five minutes at a time.'

'I know. It's a dead loss.'

'Tell me, Chrissie, could the boat sink?'

'Of course she could. All boats can sink, big or small. She's wallowing now, I can feel it. Of course the deeper she sits in the water, the more the busted seams in the hull are exposed.'

'And if she went down?'

'We don't have a dinghy, as you can see. Or nearly enough life-belts. Our best chance would be to transfer everyone to another vessel. But we've not come to that yet. I still intend to get her home. We're about two hours out of Ramsgate.'

'Of course. Is there anything else we can do?'

'There is, and let's do it now. We get under the deck and have men bailing out with anything that comes to hand. There's a couple of pots and pans in the galley. We'll need to form a human chain, passing pans of sea-water from hand to hand.'

'Let's get on it then.'

'But before that we chuck overboard everything that isn't absolutely necessary. Will you help?'

'Yes. Anything.'

Malan's eight-foot ladder was the first to go, followed by spare cans of petrol and another of water, some stuff from the galley, and the wash basin. They kept the toilet. It was the devil's own job to separate the French from their attaché cases but eventually even they went into the drink.

'Anything else?' said Chrissie when she caught up with Hardy again.

'One of these French chaps has been a real pain in the backside,' he told her. 'He's refused to be separated from any of his gear and he won't help with the pump. What say we heave him over the side?'

'You're not worried about an international incident?'

'There is that. Have you got a plank he could walk?'

'We've already thrown it out.'

'Of course you have.'

She showed Hardy how to get the bailing going and left him to it. He soon had the French hard at work, even relishing the activity after hours of sitting about. She learnt a lot from watching how he dealt with men. She could see why he'd won his captain's rank.

She got Joseph to go and help them. It was partly that she wanted to be at the wheel herself, with the space to reflect; just her, her father sleeping, the boat, the sea. It would be the last time for ages.

Chrissie jumped, feeling an arm round her shoulders. Her father had risen silently from the deck to indulge in an entirely uncharacteristic gesture. She refrained from any movement, so he wouldn't change his mind, though it didn't prevent her from scolding him.

'Is this wise, dad? You're supposed to be resting, you know.'

'I'm OK, Chrissie. Thought I'd come and see my daughter.'

'She's always pleased to see you. I hope you know that – though I sometimes wonder.'

The brief exchange – so unlike them both – derived from exceptional circumstances, she knew. They stood in silence and she thought that was the end of it. But Mr Sellick wasn't done.

'I know you think I've always favoured Tom over you but it's not straightforward, having kids. One of 'em arrives first and you get used to that and then another one comes along. Sometimes they remind you of your wife – a mixed blessing – or bloody hell, you see yourself in them, though it takes 20 years. Not that you always feel the same of course, are you crazy? You don't even like them all the time. You always love them though. You always love them.'

'I've never heard you talk so long in one go,' she told him.

He continued as if she'd not spoken. 'You'll find out when you and your young man get going.'

'He's not my young man – not yet, anyway.'

'Oh he's your young man all right. The poor lamb doesn't know what he's in for. You'll be difficult, but he won't regret a thing.'

'Thank you, father.'

The soliloquy seemed to have tired him, and with Chrissie's encouragement he sat down again, leaning against the bulwark and speaking out now and then. She poured him a drink of water and fussed over his bandages. Then stood at the wheel willing the boat onwards. She knew without looking that *Blithe Spirit* was deeper in the water, but they reached the North Goodwin lightship and she felt they'd almost made it. In that moment came the sudden realisation of her own weariness. There was even a dizzy spell and she gripped the wheel to keep herself upright.

Hardy stuck his head through the door to ask if everything was all right.

'Is the bailing OK?' she asked.

'It's fine. Joseph's taken over. He's got it going like clockwork.'

'Can you stay and talk? I feel I'm going to fall asleep at the wheel.'

'Not surprising after all you've done.'

She nodded towards the cabin. 'This isn't what I signed up for, you know, bringing a boat-full of Frenchmen to England.'

'The French have had a bad press,' Hardy admitted. 'Some of it's deserved – they were wildly unrealistic in the beginning – but they've also been heroic.'

'*Have* they!'

'They made a brave stand at Lille to keep the Boche off the perimeter. Same thing at Bray Dunes. Their defence of Calais and Boulogne was amazing, by all accounts. Don't believe everything you hear on the grapevine. It's their country, we shouldn't forget. They must be desolate. Hard for us islanders to understand.'

'I suppose.'

'They have their grievances too. General Gort promised three British divisions would screen the withdrawal from Dunkirk. The promise hasn't been honoured by the new chap.'

'I see. You believed in Gort?'

He nodded. 'It'll take 50 years for his reputation to be restored.'

She liked having Hardy there. He was the first man she'd met with a broad understanding of the war. All the same her spirits were at a low ebb. She was thinking about Tyler, about Arthur, maimed for life. She was thinking about *Blithe Spirit* at the bottom of the sea.

'Has there been any point to all this?' she said. 'All these men and ships. All this dreadful waste.'

'You mustn't think like that, Chrissie. War's a waste all right. I'm the first to admit it and I'm a soldier. But this evacuation is taking three hundred thousand British troops out of German hands. One day they'll go back, god willing. It's much more than that though. You saw the scenes at Ramsgate harbour. Britain's alive again. Not just the troops, but every man and woman in the country. As for you and your dad – you've actually been part of it.'

Again she felt grateful for Hardy's presence. There was a neatness about having him around to bestow an epilogue on their three days at sea; a full-stop to their endeavours. *She* believed in *him*. She had the absurd notion that while he was talking they'd manage to stay afloat.

'We've been a very small part,' she said, 'But will anyone know? Will people know what it was really like?'

'There'll be all sorts of stories. but don't expect the truth. Countries at war need heroes. The myth-makers are already at work.'

'But *we* know. We know what happened.'

'Yes but...' He laughed. 'How's your ship's log? Is it up-to-date?'

She laughed with him. 'We don't keep a log.'

'Of course you don't. You're too busy keeping the boat afloat. Staying alive. If people write anything, it'll be on the back of an envelope. There'll be little agreement about who did what and when and where. But you'll know and I hope you'll never forget. I've been heartened by what I've seen on this boat.' He glanced up. 'We're nearly there, by the way.'

As he spoke a mine-sweeper surged past them, closer than it should have done, and the after-swell buffeted *Blithe Spirit's* hull. What the ship was doing in that location she never knew, because it certainly wasn't making for Ramsgate's harbour. Afterwards she was inclined to blame herself for the incident, though there was little she could have done about it.

Ten minutes later they were tied up at the quay in Ramsgate harbour. Unsurprisingly, the first person they saw there was Malan. The paramedics came onto the boat and took away the wounded Frenchmen. They insisted on taking Mr Sellick too, though he resisted hard.

'Make him go with you,' Chrissie told the medics. And to her father, 'I'll find you in the triage tent.'

Someone from the Free French movement was at hand and took charge of the troops who weren't injured. One by one they shook Chrissie's hand and thanked her.

Hardy also shook hands, with Joseph – again – and then with Chrissie. 'Be prepared,' he told her, 'You're going to feel very down for a while. I just want to say – you inspire me.'

Though busy, the quayside was less frantic than before because very little was going out. Chrissie felt at a loss as to her next move, until Malan took her aside. He cast a dubious eye on *Blithe Spirit*, sagging in the water.

'You've got problems there, my girl.'

'The troops have been bailing, but now...'

'Do me a favour, will you, and get her away from the quayside. And quick.'

'As bad as that?'

'I hope I'm wrong.'

'I could go back out of the harbour and run it onto the sands.'

He gave her an old-fashioned look. 'Do you feel like a swim, then?'

'Oh!'

She'd kept the engines running, so turned the boat round and took her to a corner of the harbour, next to a flight of steps. Joseph was by her side and offered to keep bailing, but she told him not to bother.

She moored her, and stood with Joseph at the foot of the steps looking on. She'd expected the removal of 25 men from the decks to buy some time, but it seemed to have the opposite effect. How much their close encounter with the minesweeper was responsible she was never to know. *Blithe Spirit* was barely recognisable as the sprightly vessel of Chrissie's waking dreams; she sulked in the water, turning her back on the owner who doted on her.

'Why don't you come away now?' Joseph urged.

Chrissie shook her head. 'I'll stay with her to the end.'

'But it's so awful for you.'

'I won't embarrass you, Jos. I never cry. Keep me company, if you don't mind.'

It could have been ten minutes, maybe more. The boat gave a curious sucking sound, like someone struggling for breath, and shook all over. There was just one plangent squeal as the ropes parted, then she descended with graceful acceptance into the final embrace of the sea.

~ Epilogue ~

'You could come back to the house again,' Chrissie told Joseph, 'If you'd like to.'

'Thanks but it would only put off the inevitable. I need to get on one of these special trains. The military police are lurking, ready to jump on any backsliders. We'll be taken off to a camp and made into proper soldiers. But I'll be back, Chrissie.'

'You'd bloody well better be.'

They didn't kiss. He said a chaste goodbye, touching her arm, and went off to his fate. Chrissie walked away from the harbour without looking back. Her father was waiting in the triage tent, with a fresh dressing on his shoulder. He barely reacted when she described *Blithe Spirit's* final moments.

'The doctor thought you'd done a good job on me,' he said. 'I'm in the clear, apparently. Just need to get the dressing changed in a couple of days.'

With dusk coming down, they walked home side by side through the familiar streets. Chrissie felt the ground shift beneath her feet as she accustomed herself to dry land. Buildings looked cramped after the open vistas of the sea.

At 150 High Street, Mrs Sellick was busy with dustpan and brush. She received her husband and daughter as if they'd returned from a normal day's work.

'You've just missed Stephen,' she told them. 'He called to tell us Tom's OK.'

'Thank god,' said Mr Sellick.

'How wonderful,' said Chrissie.

'There was some kind of hold-up. He couldn't give details. Tom should be home in a couple of days.'

'Thank god,' Mr Sellick repeated.

'So you're back,' said his wife. 'Have you two done enough sailing now?'

'For the time being,' said Mr Sellick. '*Blithe Spirit's* at the bottom of the harbour.'

'I suppose I should be grateful for small mercies,' his wife said. 'If you're hungry I can do the pair of you some scrambled eggs.'

'Eggs!' exclaimed Chrissie.

'Mrs Tomlin dropped them in. You know she keeps chickens.'

'That'd be very welcome,' said Mr Sellick.

'Yes please,' said Chrissie.

Mr Sellick selected an armchair to 'take the load off', and Chrissie followed suit. When Mrs Sellick returned from the kitchen ten minutes later, carrying a tray with two platefuls of scrambled eggs, her husband and daughter were both asleep.

She put the tray down and gazed for a moment at their recumbent figures. 'It's a good thing you've done out there,' she said quietly. 'I'm proud of you both.'

~ The end ~

If you liked this book, please feel free to like our page on Facebook.

A note on sources

Ramsgate and the approach of war

Simon Garfield. *We are at war*, Ebury Press, 2009. The 1940 diaries of five British citizens reporting their thoughts on the early stages of WW2.

Vince Runacre. *Then & now: Ramsgate*, The History Press, 2008. Early photographs of Ramsgate scenes matched with the same scenes today.

Michael's Bookshop, 72 King Street, Ramsgate CT11 8NY, has published many works on Ramsgate history, including: *Ramsgate for 1934* (holiday guide), and *Midst bands and bombs*, 1946, and *Ramsgate 1939 ordnance survey map*.

Ramsgate's Maritime Museum has much valuable information, and

Ramsgate Tunnels is also of interest.

Naval *and* military history

Max Hastings. *All hell let loose: the world at war 1939-1945*, Harper Press, 2012. A one-volume history of WW2.

Sinclair McKay. *Dunkirk: from disaster to deliverance, testimonies of the last survivors*, Aurum Press, 2015.

Joshua Levine. *Forgotten voices: Dunkirk*, Ebury Press, 2011. Brief extracts of testimony from survivors, arranged in chronological sequence.

Walter Lord. *The miracle of Dunkirk*, Allen Lane, 1983. Scissors and paste job drawing from the literature. Has the best maps.

Wikipedia. *Dunkirk evacuation*, 2016. A useful brief summary.

Naval history

I am grateful to my friend Iain Dewar for answering my many questions about boats and for reading the finished typescript and making numerous helpful suggestions for improvements.

A D Divine. *Dunkirk*, Faber, 1945. A superb account of the naval aspects, incorporating the testimony of numerous participants, plus clear-headed analysis of events by the author.

W J R Gardner. *The evacuation from Dunkirk: 'Operation Dynamo', 26 May - 4 June 1940*, Routledge, 2000. The official record of the naval contribution, with much important detail.

Christian Brann. *The little ships of Dunkirk*, Collectors Books Limited, 1989. Covers the 100-plus 'little ships' that were still around in 1990, with photographs, technical details, and descriptions of their Dunkirk experiences.

The motorboat and yachting manual, Temple Press, 1954. Technical details on the construction of small boats.

M J Rantzen. *Little ships handling: motor vessels*, Herbert Jenkins, 1966.

Obituary of Vic Viner, beach-master, *The Guardian*, 4 October 2016.

Military history

I am grateful to my friend Luke Smith for his helpful advice on military matters.

Gun Buster. *Return via Dunkirk*, Windrow & Greene, 1994. Account of the Dunkirk experience by an officer from a gun battery.

Jerry Murland. *Retreat and rearguard: Dunkirk 1940*, Pen & Sword, 2016. Account of different aspects of the retreat to Dunkirk by a military historian.

Basil Bartlett. *My first war: an army officer's journal for May 1940, through Belgium to Dunkirk,* Chatto & Windus, 1940. Eccentric 'collection of impressions' by a Field Security officer.

Frank Melling. *Memorable motorcycles: BSA M20 Despatch*, http://www.motorcycle-usa.com/2012.

*** *** ***

Another WW2 story from the same author, available on Kindle:

Pilot error, by David Spiller

Chris Nash is 20 years old before he discovers that his real father was a WW2 pilot killed in a flying accident two decades earlier. With the help of his father's former friends and colleagues he pieces together the story of the little-known incident. Then he meets the woman who seduced his father two days before he died, and she tells him something that plays havoc with the lives of his whole family.

Some reviews from Kindle readers

Having read many great books about flying in the war, I have decided that all the best ones (of which this is definitely one) deal as much with the emotional and social effects of the war as they do with the bravery and sacrifice shown by so many. *Tommyr*

Very good. As an ex-RAF regular I enjoyed the story very much and think it was well written. *Pete*

Absolutely brilliant. I loved every page and read it in just a few days. *V.Gorman*

An extremely well told story with all the twists of an accomplished storyteller who is very knowledgeable about aircraft and the RAF. *Dunfaxin*

A masterpiece. Beautifully crafted and moving. Read it in one sitting and loved it. *Geoff Hill*

One of the best books I have read in a long time. Well written, good characterisation and a gripping plot. *Alec F.*

Absolutely superb. Have read it twice and will again. Highly recommended. *Amazon customer*

A totally compelling read. *Autopilot*

I have a soft spot for this book. Brilliant story line and exciting all the while. *The lodger*

*** *** ***

Another WW2 story from the same author, available on Kindle:

Out of Burma by David Spiller

When the Japanese bombed Rangoon in 1942, British forces fell back into northern Burma, and half a million members of the unpopular Indian community set out on the thousand-mile journey back to India. Jean Costain, young wife of a British intelligence officer, joined the exodus, along with her beautiful Indian maid and the maid's 11-year old daughter. They travelled by Jeep, paddle-steamer and on foot through inhospitable jungle, facing hunger, disease, gangs of deserters, and the Japanese. They mixed with British troops engaged in the longest fighting retreat in their history. On the way, Jean discovered much about her own resourcefulness, her attitudes to race and class, and her capacity for love.

Some reviews from Kindle readers

Having recently read Viscount Slim's biography we greatly enjoyed this well-written novel. It proved not only to be a well-written story but also clearly based on sound background research. *Peterwot*

Excellent story, well written and totally absorbing. Could not put it down. *Al P*

Unbelievable story of hardship and determination *Radiomem*

Printed in Great Britain
by Amazon

56782705R00088